MW01229410

## ALSO BY CATHY PERKINS

The Professor

Honor Code

Cypher

So About the Money

Malbec Mayhem

# Double Down

## CATHY PERKINS

ISBN 10: 1-942003072
ISBN 13: 9781942003076

Red Mountain Publishing
Cover by Gwen Phifer Campbell-Cook

Printed in the United States of America

# DOUBLE DOWN

Murder isn't supposed to be in the cards for blackjack dealer Maddie Larsson. Dealing cards at the Tom Tom Casino isn't her dream job, but it pays better than anything else she's currently qualified to do. Busted takes on a new meaning, however, when her favorite customer, a former Poker World Tour champion, is murdered. His family claims—loudly and often—that Maddie is a gold-digging murderer. She better prove she's on the level before the real killer cashes in her chips.

If the victim's body had been dumped five hundred yards up the road, Franklin County Sheriff's Detective JC Dimitrak wouldn't have been assigned to the Tom Tom Casino murder case. Instead, he's hunting for suspects and evidence while dealing with a nemesis from the past and trying to preserve his own future. He better play his cards correctly and find the killer before an innocent woman takes the ultimate hit.

# PRAISE FOR CATHY PERKINS' NOVELS

Cathy Perkins is one of those authors whose talent you spot immediately and latch onto as she becomes one of your must-reads. Her Holly and JC are fun (and hot) in *So About the Money* and you'll not only laugh and enjoy the ride, you'll be looking Perkins up to see what else she has out right now.

~ *Toni McGee Causey, bestselling author of the Bobbie Faye series*

"...an entertaining read, filled with funny snappy dialogue." ~ *RT Review*

CPA Holly Price juggles dodgy clients, flakey parent, ex-lovers and a murdered friend before she gets to the bottom line in this fast and fun read.

~ *Patricia Smiley, bestselling author of Cool Cache*

# Double Down

**Cathy Perkins**

# CHAPTER ONE

*Thursday*

Two, six, four, three, seven. Madeline Larsson spun the cards across the green felt of the casino's blackjack table. She took in the sequence and suppressed a flinch. Even the cards were mocking her.

Twenty six thousand, four hundred thirty seven dollars. She held her hands steady as she flipped a second card to each player. Her mind still reeled like a drunken fan watching Sunday sports in the Tom Tom's bar. The university's finance officer had been matter of fact when he dropped the bombshell—the total cost for full-time student status. Her despair must have leaked through her smile. He'd added she "might" qualify for financial aid.

Rolling through the hand on autopilot, she peeked at the players arrayed before her, scanning their body language and expressions. Three men, one woman. They were having a ho-hum night, which probably meant "no tip for Maddie."

Stay positive.

For a Thursday night, four at her table was a good showing.

Good was a relative term, of course. The Tri-

Cities of Washington state—Richland, Kennewick and Pasco—weren't exactly Las Vegas, and the Tom-Tom Casino definitely wasn't the Bellagio. Still, it was a nice looking place. Rows of slot machines bordered the card portion. Leather upholstered stools snugged up to the semi-circular tables. Overhead, nets of small white lights blanketed the ceiling, mimicking a star-studded sky. The twinkling lights effectively hid the ductwork and industrial part of the place.

She checked bets for a new hand and slipped cards from the shoe, dealing two cards to each person.

Staying positive was tough when even her part-time student tuition bill hung over her head. Too many of her high school friends were drowning in student debt. She'd vowed not to fall into that trap. Instead, she'd taken extra shifts, but her parents had jobs too. Even they had limits on how often they could take care of Caden. Trusting a sitter with her son for the late hours at the casino wasn't an option.

Two busts, a tie and a win for the female player. She collected cards and distributed chips.

She wouldn't be twenty-something and pretty forever, able to pull in large tips. But missing a semester of school wasn't an option either. A degree would open doors, offer a more secure job and a future for her son. She brightened her smile and hoped one of the players had a good enough—there was that relative term again—evening that they remembered to tip her.

The guy at the end had a terrible hand, a two and a three. All evening he'd made only the minimum bet, spiked by random long shots that split about fifty/fifty in paying off. With a quick glance at his current cards, he surrendered, retrieving a portion of his ante.

She worked past the next two players. One bust. One sticking at nineteen. As she turned to the last man, she noticed Frank Phalen lurking beyond her table. She didn't know the security chief well. Deeply tanned with dark hair brushing his collar, Frank wore jeans, a fringe-trimmed shirt, and a cowboy hat with an intricate turquoise band. Nothing overtly scary, but everything about him shouted "intense."

She'd been vaguely aware of his presence since her shift began. Tension tightened her shoulders but she focused on the player in front of her. The guy had been making wild crazy bets since he sat down. This hand was no exception. With a pair of tens, instead of sticking with a conservative, probably winning hand, he'd split and doubled down, apparently hoping for face cards for the draw.

Frank shifted, distracting her. She'd heard the stories about him obsessing over women. One had taken out a restraining order against him. Another rumor had him involved with a woman who'd been murdered last month. A shudder shimmied up her spine.

Go away.

She didn't need another overbearing man complicating her life. Asher already had that covered—in spades.

Two cards slid across the table to the crazy player. An eight to give him eighteen for one bet and a six for sixteen on the other.

His fingers hovered above the cards.

Don't do it.

Drawing against a soft sixteen was a sucker

move.

He tapped the six. "Hit me."

She pulled another card for him. Six of clubs. Busted at twenty-two.

With two gamblers still in play, she glanced at her own cards. A player sitting at nineteen meant she— as the casino—needed at least a nineteen to tie. No one "won" on the tie, but the casino didn't lose any money paying on the bet either. Her hole card was a jack with a four showing. A fourteen required her to take another card. A six joined the four. Suppressing a smile, she flipped the downward facing card. "Twenty," she announced and cleared the table.

The crazy guy slammed back against his seat. Red splotches lit his neck.

Maddie hoped a new hand would move him past the loss. "Place your—"

Frank moved in beside the angry man. A security pair stepped up to the guy seated on the end. Maddie gave Frank a sharp glance and bit off the rest of her words. His words were quiet but she caught them. "Do not make a scene. Gather your belongings. Card counting is not allowed and you know it."

She tightened her jaw before her mouth could sag open. *That* was why Frank had been hovering. He hadn't been watching *her*. He'd been watching the *players*, cheaters in the casino's eyes.

Wow, card counters. She should've picked up on the betting pattern. After dealing for countless hours, she instinctively knew what cards were still in the shoe. She gave herself a mental shake. Quit worrying about school and how to pay for it. Get your head in the game.

The red-faced man opened his mouth, a protest

sputtering out in a spray of spit. The guy at the end shrank, as if he could sink into the floor and disappear. In unison, the security team clamped hands on the men's upper arms.

Action stopped at the surrounding tables. The gamblers watched, open-mouthed, while the dealers tried to reclaim their attention.

"Let's go." Frank's voice was as steely as any police officer's.

The group shuffled away and Maddie glanced at the remaining players. Fascinated shock splayed across the woman's features. The last guy rose, winked and slid a chip toward her. His behavior flashed across her mind as he moved in the opposite direction from security. Purposeful but discrete, he walked with the same under-the-radar style he'd displayed at the gaming table. Now that she thought about it, he'd been counting cards as well, but using the more obvious, inexperienced guys for cover. She turned to signal security, glanced back, but the guy was already gone.

"Well. That was different." The woman gathered her chips and also slid one forward for Maddie. "I think I'll call it a night."

Maddie smiled her thanks while scanning the casino for possible players. Having the entire table empty wasn't the way to attract people. It screamed both "problem" and "cold table."

The gamblers at the surrounding tables turned back to their cards, as if the scene were part of the evening entertainment. The other dealers kept their focus on their own tables. She wasn't sure if it was deliberately distancing themselves from a train wreck or making sure their own charges weren't cheating.

An empty table.

Keeping a warm smile pasted on her lips, she let her eyes drift over the crowd, looking for the pit boss. It was almost time for her break. She could use the rotation of dealers as a way to attract a new group of gamblers afterward. Just as she located the pit boss, a man dropped into one of the chairs.

"Daniel." The warmth in her voice was real. The old man came into the casino often and always sat at her table.

He dropped some cash on the table.

Maddie tucked the currency into the drop box and pulled chips from the rack. As Daniel Kaufman placed his first bet, she automatically slid two cards across the table and dealt her own.

A two and a ten for Daniel. She had a five showing. Her hole card was probably a face card. Not that she was counting or anything.

Daniel's lucky charm appeared—a World Poker Tour championship chip. A nick marred the bold blue border surrounding the tour's logo. A chip in the chip. Her smile broadened. An image of Daniel clenching the disc in his teeth, testing it like gold, immediately surfaced. One day she'd ask him how he'd damaged it.

He rolled the chip across his knuckles like a coin, then tapped the uppermost card. "Hit me."

A five joined the twelve he had showing. With a laugh, he waved her off. "What do you have?"

She flipped over a queen to pair with her five, and then threw a seven to bust. She slid chips to Daniel and cleared the table. "You okay? What did you do to your eye?" A yellowing bruise marred the left side of his face.

Daniel sighed and looked away. His sigh ended in a deep cough, a rattling, rasping sound that would've made Maddie haul Caden into the pediatrician's office. With Daniel's cough, she would've called it a smoker's cough—they still had too many smokers in the casino—except she knew Daniel didn't smoke.

"It's time for my break. I could use a soda. Come on. Join me." Maddie signaled the pit boss. A moment later, another dealer stepped up to the table.

Maddie led the way to the snack bar. Minutes later, they were seated at a small table tucked into the far corner of the lounge. "What happened?"

"Why can't that kid be more like his older brother? Or like you? Look at you. Working. Going to school and taking care of your son."

"This isn't about me. If you don't want to talk about it, that's fine."

He stared into his drink and swirled the scotch over the ice cubes.

She sipped her soda and waited, quietly studying the older man. Beyond the black eye, his color looked bad. Now that he was still, without the usual animation lighting his face, she noticed the fatigue and sheen of perspiration. "Is your insomnia kicking in?" teetered at the edge of her tongue.

"My youngest, Owen, hit me up for money again." The words were abrupt. He still wasn't looking at her.

She joined his wince at the word choice.

"I'd had it with him. Had a Come to Jesus session about working and responsibility." Daniel's fingers gingerly poked his face. "He didn't take it well."

"I'm sorry. Is that why you haven't been in this week?" Stress, she decided. It did bad things to your body.

Daniel nodded. "I had some decisions to make. About me. About the kids. The older three are fine. Ryan works hard. He's got a good job, a nice place for his family. My daughter's able to work part time while her kids are in school. Her husband's got a steady job. Same for Jeremy. So how in the hell did Owen end up such a slacker?"

Maddie shook her head. "Asher's the same way. Always an excuse why something—a job, a class, you name it—wasn't working for him. I made the mistake of pointing out the operative word was 'work.'" Asher had hauled off and hit her too. She should've thrown him out then. Part of their divorce decree had been a restraining order that mandated he couldn't see her—or Caden—unless he participated in AA. He'd been pretty consistent until last week when he'd fallen off the wagon. She rubbed the bruise on her forearm. It was still sore where he'd grabbed her when he showed up drunk last week.

"Yeah. It's like the kid expects me to support his lazy ass instead of getting out there to earn his own." Daniel took a long swallow of his drink, then carefully positioned the glass in the center of the napkin. "Look, I wouldn't have said anything except...well...I made the mistake of using you as an example since he's tired of hearing about 'Saint Ryan.' Owen made some...wild accusations."

"About...?"

"You and me. Mostly you. I don't think he'd do anything, but I wanted to warn you."

"He threatened me? My job? My family? My

8

*child?*" Her voice rose as outrage warred confusion.

"No, no, no." Daniel made patting gestures with his hands. "Nothing like that. He.... He claimed you were 'after' me. That you were after my money."

Heat flooded her cheeks. "I never—"

"I know you didn't—you wouldn't—but in case Owen shows up here looking for me. Says something." He lifted one shoulder. "Causes a scene. I wanted you to be prepared."

"How do you prepare for something like that?"

# CHAPTER TWO

Maddie crossed the casino's parking lot, headed for the employee section. Security lights brightened the area, but the acre of empty asphalt mocked the solitary click of her high heels. *Head on a swivel.* How many times had security—and her dad—hammered that lesson at her? Always be aware of your surroundings.

Like the original Tom Tom casino in Kennewick, the Tom Tom Two was located in a commercial area of Pasco. Except for the car dealerships further down Highway 395, the surrounding businesses closed early. At 3 AM, the road fronting the casino was quiet, with only an occasional car sweeping past. Faint traffic noise drifted in from the interstate spur, a hum that would ordinarily be buried under everyday sounds. She swept her gaze over the parking lot. *Click, click.* Her shoes marked her progress. She might hear another woman in heels approaching her.

But what about a guy?

Her head turned, left, right. Her gaze probed the shadows around the parked cars. This was the worst part of the job.

Only a few cars remained in the employee lot.

Not many people worked the late night shift. Several vehicles clustered near the casino's entrance, the night-owl gamblers who tended to stick to the electronic games. Juggling her purse and a birthday present the casino manager had given her for Caden, she pointed the key fob at her car and chirped the door open.

She sank into the driver's seat of the Civic and with a groan, kicked off her shoes. Standing on her feet all night was killer, even if the heels did make her legs look great. How did the older women do this? No wonder most of the dealers were young.

She dropped the present and her purse on the passenger seat, stuck the key in the ignition and cranked.

And cranked.

"Come on. Start."

Whine, *grrrr*. Whine, *grrrr*.

"Please start."

A faint odor of gas reached her. Great. Asher had yelled at her before about flooding the engine. Whatever that meant. Flooded with gas? Was that even possible?

Whatever. Now she'd have to wait until the fuel cleared.

If the car wouldn't start, how would she get home? She reached for her phone, then hesitated. Who could she call at this time of night? Waking up the entire house by calling her parents would be a recipe for disaster. Even her friends from the casino would be asleep by now.

Damn, she needed to get home. She'd planned to leave Caden at her parents' house for the night. That way, she'd at least get a couple hours of sleep before she put Party Central plans in high gear. Friday would be a blur of birthday cake baking, decorating, and keeping Caden from bouncing off the walls until a dozen four-year-olds showed up on Saturday morning.

Hopefully Asher would remember to show up for the party. It wouldn't be the first time he'd disappointed Caden—she was so past being disappointed by anything he did—but really? One day of the year you'd think Asher could do the right thing.

She turned the key again. Whine, *grrrr*.

"Start, dammit!" She banged her fist against the steering wheel as if that would knock something loose.

Not tonight. Her head drooped against the car seat.

Motion across the parking lot caught her attention. A man emerged from the entrance and turned in her direction.

Damn. Employee or player?

She craned her neck. Please be someone I know. Someone who knows how to make a car start.

Most of the people she knew had left hours ago. She'd stayed for the extra hours tonight in an attempt to make up for missing her regular Friday night shift.

A cowboy hat shaded the man's face. Who did she know that wore one? Most guys in the area wore ball caps.

A number of the Hispanic players wore cowboy hats. Don't be a gambler. The last thing she needed was having to deal with a strange man in the middle of the night in a deserted parking lot.

No need to panic. Her car always started.

Eventually.

Whine, *grrrrr*.

The guy was headed straight toward her.

Please be going home. Do not come over here. She tugged her purse closer and fished for her phone. If he did anything sketchy, she was calling the cops.

She squinted at the man as he passed under a lamppost. Wait a minute. It looked like...it was...the security chief.

"Car trouble?" Frank Phalen stopped about three feet from the car.

Relief drained tension from her shoulders. But still... Awkward. She barely knew him. And there were those rumors about him being creepy.

He was the head of security. Surely she could trust him.

She toggled the window switch. "No. Maybe. It won't start. I think I flooded it." Ugh. Seriously? She was parroting Asher.

"Turn on your lights."

She flipped the switch and two pools of light flooded the casino's stucco wall.

"Not your battery. Try it again. Hold the accelerator all the way down. If it's flooded that should clear it."

Whine, *grrrrr*.

Frank tilted the cowboy hat back on his head. "Pop the hood."

Release switch...She swayed back and forth, peering into the foot well. The release switch was down there somewhere. She mashed a button and the trunk lid flipped open. Oops. Her cheeks warmed.

Frank didn't say a word. Maybe he wasn't such a

13

jerk. At least he knew when to keep quiet.

She grabbed her phone, punched the flashlight app and aimed it at the pedals. *There.* An icon of a car with the hood raised gleamed from a button.

The hood lifted a few inches and Frank fiddled with the catch until the hood opened. He leaned over the engine compartment. A minute later, he slammed the hood and stepped closer to the window. "I don't see a loose connection. The battery works, so it probably isn't the alternator. It may be something with your starter or electronic ignition. That'd be a lot less expensive than the mother board going out."

She heard. *Mwahmwahmwah.* Battery. *Mwahmwahmwah.* Expensive.

"I can call a tow truck for you. Do you have a preferred garage?"

Mine probably wasn't the right answer. "Asher, my ex-husband, always handled the car."

Wow, but did she suddenly feel incompetent.

"I think he took it to the dealer." She chewed her lip. Frustrated despair roiled her stomach. Car repair. Finding a mechanic. Arrange a loaner car. Not another item for her ginormous To Do list. There weren't enough hours in the day or night.

And, oh dear God, the money...

Apparently her tuition saving account was about to take a serious hit.

"Do you have AAA or another service?"

She shook her head, willing herself not to cry.

"This time of night." Frank scratched his temple. "Look. I can call the tow company the casino has a contract with. It'll be a lot less expensive for you, but they'll take it to their shop instead of the dealer."

Hoping she wasn't being completely naive, she

blinked back tears. "Thanks. Less expensive is good."

He pulled out a phone, tapped around, then stepped away to talk to someone, apparently the tow service. Phone pressed to his ear, he retraced his steps toward her car. "Not an impound. One of our employees needs your mechanic to take a look at her car."

A moment later, he tucked the phone back into his pocket. "The overnight guy is on a call, but dispatch will send him over as soon as he gets back. I'll wait until he gets here."

"Thanks." She was starting to feel like a broken record. With a glance at the package in the passenger seat, she asked, "Do you want to sit down?"

"Okay." He strolled around the back of the car and casually closed the trunk as he passed.

Her face burned.

She swept the birthday present and her purse into the back seat. The passenger door clicked closed, making her too aware of a strange man sitting beside her.

The silence stretched. Small talk was a staple for a dealer. Quick small talk. Not fill up time waiting for a tow truck talk. Soooo. "Are you from the Tri-Cities?"

"Seattle. I moved here about a year ago." He settled the cowboy hat in his lap.

"I've been at the Tom Tom for nearly three years, so I knew you started working here earlier this year. Were you at one of the Seattle casinos? Muckleshoot? Tulalip?"

He shook his head. There was a long pause, then he said, "I was a police officer."

She blinked. The tension in his posture told her

15

# CATHY PERKINS

not to ask why he wasn't working in law enforcement. "Well, I'm glad you were here tonight. You rescued me."

"How'd you end up working here?" He tilted his head, indicating the casino.

How to answer? She chewed her lip. "I needed a job with evening hours. With tips, this pays better than most places. I have a second job during the day that fits around Caden's pre-school and my class schedule."

He turned and studied her. "You're working two jobs and going to school?"

She couldn't read his expression. Was that skepticism or admiration? "The second job and school are part-time."

He nodded and continued to study her.

She squirmed under his scrutiny. No way did she want to still be working this job five years from now. "When my son starts school, I want a job with more predictable hours."

There. That sounded mature without offering any details. Determined to place the attention back on him, she asked, "Did you grow up in Seattle?"

"Maple Valley. Went to U Dub and then joined SPD."

She interpreted, Seattle suburb, University of Washington, Seattle Police Department. Why on earth had he left with those roots?

"You at Washington State here?" He ran a thumb along the cowboy hat's brim.

"Community college for now." It was less expensive. "But my grades are good. I want to transfer next fall for my junior year." That way her degree would be from the university, which carried

16

more weight with potential employers.

"If your grades are good, have you looked at scholarships? Might let you ease up on the second job."

"Aren't scholarships just for high school kids?" She and Asher had married right after she graduated. He'd dropped out of Washington State and come back to Kennewick to work. A fact he'd thrown in her face a million times, whenever he bitched about the latest crummy job he'd had to take since he didn't have a degree. She'd worked retail until Caden was born. Asher wanted her to stay home afterward, but the stress of a newborn plus the loss of her paycheck had sent him—and their marriage—completely over the cliff.

"No clue." Frank shrugged. "Couldn't hurt to check."

He had a nice smile. And he didn't seem to be laughing at her for trying to create a better life the way Asher did. "I'll add it to the To Do List."

"With how many thousands of other items?" The smile deepened to a full grin.

They talked about colleges and classes until the tow truck rumbled into the parking lot. Frank immediately shifted into security chief mode and stepped out of her car. Maddie figured she should stand up and deal with the driver herself, but she was exhausted. It was nice to have someone else handle the mess.

The driver backed the tow truck toward her car, then stepped out and talked to Frank.

She grabbed her purse and Caden's birthday present, then remembered the party supplies in the trunk. Plus she'd forgotten all about needing a cab.

"Guys?" The men looked up from whatever they were doing to attach her car to the tow truck. "What cab company does the casino use? I need to arrange a ride."

"I can drop you at your house." The tow truck driver wiped his hands on a rag.

"I'll take her home." Frank sent a quelling look at the driver.

"Really, that isn't necessary." Although it would beat standing around waiting for a cab to show up. "You've been super helpful already."

"Maddie." Her name emerged on an exaggerated patient sigh.

How did he know her nickname?

"You're a valued employee. It's nearly four in the morning. From the kid's present you're lugging around plus all the decorating junk, I'm guessing you have a party to attend or arrange. Let's not waste time discussing this."

"How..." D'oh! The open trunk he'd closed. And he was right. It was pointless to turn down the offer. "Thanks."

He jogged across the lot to a black Jeep. The tow driver waited beside his truck while Frank angled in beside her car and helped her transfer the party supplies.

Moments later, her car was riding away from the casino and Maddie was perched awkwardly on the front seat of Frank's Jeep.

"Where are we going?"

The reality of her car disappearing down Court Street hit her. What was she going to do without a car this weekend? Picking up Caden. All the errands she still needed to take care of before the party.

Oh, crap. She'd have to ask if she could borrow her mother's car. Which meant she'd have to call a cab and be at their house early enough to pick up Caden and take her mother to work.

Or she could go with Plan B. Tomorrow—later today—was going to be long enough. She could crash on her parents' couch. No sense adding the expense of a cab ride.

One step at a time. The mantra had brought her this far.

She rattled off her parents' address.

"Your kid?" Frank tilted his head at the pile of paper goods, balloons, and craft supplies. A plastic fire truck sat on top of the heap.

"My son will be four."

"He likes fire trucks?"

"Loves them."

"A couple friends of mine are firefighters. If they don't have a call-out, I can ask them if they'll do a drive-by. Let the kids crawl around on the rig."

She stared at him. "You—they—would do that?"

"Sure."

"That would be awesome."

Clearly the rumors about him were wrong. He was a nice guy. Too bad she didn't have an older sister to introduce him to.

# CHAPTER THREE

*Friday night*

Franklin County Sheriff's Detective JC Dimitrak stopped in front of a two-story house. The place looked like every other new home built during northern Pasco's wild growth spurt. His gaze tracked across the exterior. There was the requisite three-car garage, with the cars parked in the driveway because the garage bays were full of junk. Beige siding, white trim. On the upside, a bit of fake rock anchored the columns at the entrance. The bushes across the front said someone was trying to take care of the yard.

He checked in with Dispatch, stalling as long as he could. He'd already noticed the twitch in the front window curtains. Someone was home, wondering who he was. Friday evening, dinnertime. Lights were on inside the house, filtering to the front from what was most likely a family room/kitchen at the rear of the residence.

Hopefully both of the Kaufmans were present. He'd called Ryan Kaufman at the auto dealership, thinking he might catch the guy there. The receptionist said he'd already left. Daniel Kaufman's phone had Ryan as the designated contact, but several other people were in the favorites section.

They might also be family members. If Ryan wasn't home, he'd move to the next name on the victim's list.

Damn, he hated notification calls.

If the killer had dumped the body five hundred yards up the road, a Pasco investigator would be sitting here instead of him. JC took a deep breath, trying to both remember and dismiss the mental images of the crime scene. No crime scene was pretty. This one, after the body cooked inside the car for a day, had been especially brutal.

The smell, the flies...

For him, however, working the crime scene did more than provide the details of the homicide. Outrage at the killer, at the vicious, *personal* element of a gunshot to the face, lit up the private connection he felt to the victim. He stashed that anger in the section of his head—and heart—that motivated him.

Time to deal with the family. Time to start digging.

He squared his shoulders and put on his work face.

Time to find justice for a dead man.

But first...the really shitty part.

Telling the son.

JC climbed from the unmarked and headed to the front porch. The overhead light flicked on and a woman answered the door. Brunette. About five foot, six; probably one hundred forty pounds. She wore jeans and one of those holiday themed sweaters. He introduced himself. "Is your husband home?"

A minute later he was seated in a neat den across a low table from Ryan and Emily Kaufman. He

21

studied the couple as he pulled out his notebook. On the short side, about five foot, eight, Ryan was one of those guys who still looked like a kid. Wide cheeks, bright blue eyes, patches of color on his cheeks. The open expression probably worked for him at the car dealership.

"I doubt this is a social call." Ryan leaned forward, hands clasped, forearms resting on his thighs. "What can we help you with Detective?"

"I'm sorry to inform you." JC released a sigh.

"Is there a problem?" Ryan straightened, sitting taller as if bracing himself for bad news.

"I'm here to tell you your father is dead." Just get it out there. Watch the reaction. Be the bastard in the room.

Emily gasped.

Ryan shook his head, as if rejection would undo the death. "I just talked to him. You must have the wrong person."

"When did you talk to him?"

"Wednesday evening. He goes to church with us."

"Was that the last time you saw him?"

"The last time," the woman murmured before she began to cry in earnest.

Ryan put an arm around his wife, but focused on JC. "You're sure it's Dad?"

"I'll need you to come to the morgue for official identification, but his wallet was in his pocket."

"What happened?" A faintly frantic air surrounded him. "Why are the police involved?"

"He was shot."

"What? When?" Ryan asked.

"Why?" gasped Emily.

22

"We're investigating. Anything you can tell us about him will be helpful."

Ryan surged to his feet and stormed across the room. Hands on hips, he stared out the window.

JC rose and found a box of tissues. He handed it to the wife, who gave him a watery smile. "Thank you."

Ryan whirled to face JC. "Who shot my dad?"

"We're investigating. I know this is a difficult time for you—"

"You don't know anything about me. Don't tell me you know how I feel."

JC took a deep breath. Grief showed up in all kinds of ways. Some people cried like Emily was doing. Others let anger overwhelm the shock. "You're right. I don't know you. Asking questions at a time like this can seem intrusive, but it's the only way we can help you get justice for your dad."

"Justice," Ryan muttered.

"Please sit down, Mr. Kaufman."

"Honey." Emily reached out her hand.

Ryan crossed the room and reclaimed a seat beside his wife. "Where did it happen?"

"His body was found in his car outside Pasco."

"Damn gangbangers." Ryan leapt from his seat and stomped another circuit of the room.

"Why do you say that?" So far, JC had seen nothing that suggested gang involvement.

"Those Mexican kids cause all kinds of problems. Between the vandalism and the thefts, we've had to double security at the dealership."

"I understand that's a problem. Did your father mention trouble with a gang member?"

Ryan appeared lost in his thoughts. "They

23

could've done it," he muttered.

"When was he killed?" Emily interjected.

JC was still processing Ryan's reaction, but turned to the wife. "The Medical Examiner hasn't given us a definite time of death. The preliminary estimate is late Thursday evening or Friday morning."

"Thursday?" Emily straightened. Her hands stopped shredding the soggy tissue.

"You're just now telling us?" Anger flared in Ryan's voice again.

"The car was in a parking lot behind a closed business near the airport. After it was called in this afternoon, we had to identify the body and locate next of kin."

"What the hell was he doing near the airport?"

"I hope you can tell me. Was he planning to go out of town?" That could be where the victim crossed paths with his killer. The luxury car could've triggered a car-jacking gone bad.

"Not that I know about." Ryan dropped onto the sofa and glanced at his wife. "Dad didn't say anything to you, did he?"

"No. Nothing like that."

"You said his wallet was in his pocket?" Ryan refocused on JC. "No one took his car? His money?"

"It doesn't appear to have been a robbery. We need to learn as much about the victim as possible to identity potential suspects, and then clear as many of them as we can. That way we can focus our efforts. First thing, I need to flesh out Mr. Kaufman's life. I didn't find anyone at his house or contact information for a spouse."

"My mother died several years ago."

JC made a note. "Where was he working?"

Ryan seemed to settle down as JC questioned him. "He played on the World Poker Tour before retiring a couple of years ago. Mom died right after he left the tour. He moved up here to be closer to his family."

They ran through the family connections, confirming JC's initial impressions about Daniel's phone contact list. "You're all in the area?"

"We grew up here and like it here. Dad worked at the Lab"—the research facility loosely connected to the Hanford Nuclear site—"before he made the cut to go on tour."

"No old disagreements from either his time here working or with rivals on the tour?"

Ryan shook his head. "Everybody liked Dad. He was that kind of guy."

"He was pretty young to have retired."

"He finished high in the tour rankings. If what you're asking is, was he rich? Everything's relative. He had money." Ryan paused. His eyebrows twitched as he considered his words. "There is one thing."

"Oh?" JC prompted when Ryan didn't continue.

"You said the car was 'outside Pasco.' Was it near that cheesy casino?"

"Which one?"

"The Tom Tom?" Ryan glanced at his wife.

"The Tom Tom Two." Emily wiped her nose and crumpled the tissue. "There's another one in Kennewick, near the mall."

"That's it. The Tom Tom. The second one. Anyway, Dad hung out there. I guess it was a connection to his touring days. There was this girl.

25

Do you remember her name?" He again turned to his wife.

"Maggie, Maddie. Something like that."

"Yeah. Maddie. He talked about her a lot. We didn't think much about it at first. But the longer it went on, the more she sounded like a real gold digger. What's a girl like that doing hooking up with an old guy unless she's looking for a sugar daddy?"

"Hooking up? Did he see her outside the casino?"

"I don't know. He had his own place, so it's possible. But not long ago, Dad told my brother he was leaving his money to her when he died. I admit, I was concerned she was using him. Conning him."

"Did your dad mention it to you?" Money was a powerful crime motivator.

Ryan leaned forward and rubbed his hands. "She would have the motive and opportunity. Isn't that what you guys look at? Motive and opportunity?"

Somebody's been watching too many crime shows. "Does Maddie have a last name?"

After several more rounds of questions, JC figured he had all he was going to get from the couple. According to them, Daniel Kaufman was a church-going saint with no family, business, or neighborhood issues, whose only flaw seemed to be an attraction to a young woman named Maddie.

Sure. And the SeaHawks would win the championship again this year.

"Where were you on Thursday night?"

"What?" Anger pumped red blotches onto Ryan's neck and face.

"It's a routine question. Eliminating people from consideration is as important as focusing on the right

26

suspects."

"We were setting up a promotion. I went back to work after dinner."

"What time did you get home?"

"Midnight?" Ryan's hand flicked, palm up. "A little after? Then the rest of the night, I was here, asleep."

"What about you, Mrs. Kaufman?"

"I almost feel guilty saying it, but I slept like a log that night. I've been putting in extra hours at work and between that and the kids, it must've caught up to me. I crashed after dinner and didn't move until Ryan woke me up on Friday morning."

"And that was what time?"

She looked at her husband. "About seven? It was a scramble to get the kids fed and out the door for school."

JC jotted notes. "Mr. Kaufman, if there's nothing else you can tell me, I'll have to ask you to identify the body now."

Ryan winced.

"Would you like to contact your siblings first or would you prefer to wait until you're completely certain this man is your father?"

"Don't you tell them?"

"I can. It's up to you. Generally we find family members prefer to hear the news from a relative. I'll need to talk with your brothers and sister, so I can certainly inform them at that time."

"No, I'll do it. Let me get my keys and I'll follow you to...where do we go?"

An hour later, JC led a white-faced Ryan out of the

morgue. The body hadn't been pretty after the guy was shot in the face. Sitting in a car for most of the next day hadn't improved his appearance.

"Are you okay to drive?" he asked Ryan.

"When can we bury him?"

"The autopsy will probably be tomorrow. Monday at the latest. I recommend you contact a funeral home to make final arrangements. They'll take care of transporting the body."

Ryan stopped beside his car. He grasped the receipt for his father's personal effects. He turned his hand, examining the paper as if he'd never seen it before. "You'll return these? His watch. His wallet. His *things*?"

"Right now items found on his body are considered evidence, but they will be returned to you."

"What about his tour chip?"

"Tour chip?"

Ryan's hand tightened around the receipt until his knuckles whitened. "A chip. A blue poker chip."

"There wasn't a poker chip on the list of items in his pockets. I can ask if the technicians found one in the car. Are you sure he had it with him?"

"He always carried a chip from the World Tour. From his last championship. It had the tour logo in the center."

Why would someone take that chip and not the car or wallet? JC stared, waiting for Ryan to provide the connecting link.

"Only the championship players got those chips. Dad called it his lucky charm. It was from the year he won. He made millions on that tour."

*Rich* apparently was relative. *Millions* sounded like

"rich" to him. "You care about the chip? Or the money?"

"I care about my dad." Ryan's nostrils flared and color flooded his cheeks and neck. "That win gave him enough money to come back here to his family. His real family."

# CHAPTER FOUR

*Saturday mid-day*

Maddie was corralling muddy four-year-olds when she heard the *Brrappp* of a fire truck's siren split the air. She'd listened to a dozen friends who advised active play and sugar as key ingredients for a kid's birthday party. A bounce house—a frequent suggestion—wasn't in the affordable category, so she'd gone with pragmatic. Given Caden's obsession with firemen, she'd started with the fireman version of a treasure hunt—minus smoke, open flames and any other hazard she could envision. She'd connected several hoses in the backyard and let the kids have at it. The boys had loved finding the paper flames and reducing them to sodden lumps. Then they'd turned the hoses on her, each other, and the neighbor's dog.

Fortunately she'd warned the mothers and had towels and dry clothes ready for the cake and present portion of the party. Equally fortunate, the weather had cooperated. Indian summer kept the day sunny and warm.

The siren blasted again, sounding way too close for comfort. She ran through the living room—checking for smoke alarms or flames as she went—

and peered out the front window. A fire truck laden with ladders, hoses, and firefighters pulled to the curb in front of her house. Neighbors peeked through their windows or stood on their porches and stared.

Maddie gasped as the firefighters swarmed off the truck. Surely Frank hadn't arranged...he hadn't called or said a word...

OMG, was this for Caden?

She flung open the door and ran down the walkway.

One of the firefighters motioned to her. "Excuse me, ma'am. We have a report of a serious issue concerning a young man's heart condition."

She screeched to a halt. Heart condition? What? Wait.

"Seems his loyalty is with Emergency Services. We're here to assess his readiness for auxiliary training."

"You lost me here." She shook her head.

A grin split the firefighter's face. "Yeah, that spiel works better with older kids. I hear your kid likes firetrucks."

"Caden *adores* you guys."

"Gotta hate that." Another guy in turnout gear sauntered up to join them.

"Can I really bring a dozen four-year-olds out here?"

"We have extensive training. We can handle any crisis."

"But can you handle a dozen four-year-olds?"

"Oh, yeah."

For the next thirty minutes, the kids swarmed the truck and the firefighters. To Maddie's relief, the

31

firefighters paired off with the children, engaging without letting them do anything disastrous, like pull a lever or drive her neighbors insane with repeated blasts of the siren. Bonus points—the kids dried off without needing a clothing change. Finally she peeled the last kid away from his new hero, thanked the crew for the millionth time, and shepherded the herd inside for a whirlwind session of cake, ice cream and presents.

The doorbell rang as Caden tore into another brightly wrapped present.

Damn. She glanced at her watch. One of the moms must be early.

Or maybe...maybe Asher actually showed up.

No mom would pick up early. It had to be Asher.

Please dear Lord, let him be sober.

She'd ream him out—and slam the door in his face—if he'd been drinking.

She really would this time. No more letting him make excuses.

She jerked open the door before she lost her nerve and found a tall, dark-haired stranger standing on her porch. "Who...You're not Asher."

This guy was definitely not Asher. This guy had cornered the market on tall, dark and handsome.

"No." The man smiled, a dimple erasing years from his apparent age.

Behind him, the firefighters had finished packing up the gear they'd hauled out for the kids. One or two stood in the yard, clearly curious, while the rest piled into the truck. A dark gray sedan that screamed unmarked cop car was parked in front of her neighbor's house.

She hauled her attention back to the man when

he hauled out a badge case. "Madeline Larsson?"

She nodded.

"I'm Detective JC Dimitrak with the Franklin County Sheriff's Department."

Damn.

On so many levels.

"I'm so sorry about the noise." She gestured at the firetruck while part of her fumed. Really? One of her neighbors called the cops instead of talking with her directly or rolling for an hour with a kid's birthday party? "I didn't think it was causing that much disruption."

"You had an emergency?"

"You aren't here about the party?"

His dimple flashed again and, eyebrow raised, he turned to the firefighters. "I wasn't aware Emergency Services brought their rig to parties."

Confusion twitched her eyebrows. He didn't seem upset, like there was an emergency. "Did Frank ask you to stop by too? I mean, Caden was over the moon with the firetruck. A police officer in the same day. I may never get him out of hyperdrive."

"Who's Caden?"

The fire engine pulled away with one last blast from its siren.

"Wait." She flexed her hands, palms forward. Her attention ping-ponged between the departing firefighters and the detective. Should she wave goodbye? Call "thanks" one more time. Or deal with whatever this cop wanted. "Why are you here?"

"I need to talk with you, ask a few questions."

She glanced over shoulder, grateful there were a couple of moms in charge of the chaos in her family room. "Is everything okay with my parents? Asher didn't do something stupid, did he?"

"This is a different matter."

"Can it wait? This is a really bad time."

He raised an eyebrow again, but there was no humor in his expression this time.

"It's my son's birthday. The kids are still here."

"It's important."

"Can you come back later? The moms are supposed to be here any minute."

He hesitated, his gaze flicking past her. Kids' squeals were audible along with a crash.

With a wince, she eased the door closer, a clear signal it was time for him to leave. "I need to get back in there."

"Thirty minutes." He slid the badge into a pocket, turned and strode toward his car.

# CHAPTER FIVE

*Saturday*

JC Dimitrak noticed the fire engine as soon as he turned onto the residential street. The neighborhood was old—small houses built in the '50s when people flooded the area to work at the not-so-secret nuclear site. He rolled the unmarked sedan to a stop next door to the address Dispatch had provided for Madeline Larsson. A fire engine, swarming with firefighters, was parked in front of the target address. He toggled the laptop and scrolled through the dispatch traffic. No call for service at this location.

He parked and climbed from the unit.

Several of the firefighters paused their packing. "Yo, Dimitrak."

He lifted a hand, acknowledging guys he knew, but headed straight to the front door rather than stopping. The sooner he nailed down what this girl knew the better.

A pretty blonde with mud smears on her jeans and arm opened the door.

Mud-wrestling with the firefighters? He kept his expression neutral while he gave her a quick, assessing appraisal. Snug jeans emphasized her curvy figure, but the shirt, although wet in spots, was modest and her makeup conservative.

Anger morphed into surprise before confusion settled across her features. "You're not Asher."

Who was Asher? JC pulled out his badge case and introduced himself. She immediately started apologizing for the noise. What kind of party had the guys been part of? He'd stop by the fire station after this interview, give them some shit about the girl, and then find out what they were doing there.

Behind him the engine pulled away with a blast of the siren.

The girl, woman, Madeline, started babbling about Frank and Caden. How many guys was she involved with? Maybe Ryan Kaufman was onto something after all, although JC wasn't about to jump to conclusions. At this point Madeline was simply someone who might know the victim.

Who might have a motive to harm him.

He considered the slim file he'd accumulated on her. Young. Single mother. Part-time student. Worked at the casino the victim frequented. On the surface she checked the boxes for someone who might be looking for money. Might've taken advantage of an old man.

He started his routine. *I have questions.* He wasn't working undercover, looking to scam her into confessing. He needed to get a feel for her—whether she pinged his radar as someone who could deliberately kill an old man, or if she was merely another link in the chain that would lead him to the killer.

She interrupted with, "Can it wait? This is a really bad time."

Behind her came the unmistakable sounds of a

child's party rather than a backyard bash. He recalibrated his approach, but added, *Who did she know well enough at the firehouse for them to roll out the fire engine?* to his list of questions.

"It's my son's birthday." Her big blue eyes implored him to understand.

He hesitated. Yeah, she wasn't above using her looks to her advantage. He could push it—she was either a suspect or perhaps a material witness—but he couldn't make her talk. He had no grounds to haul her into the station. It would be better if she cooperated.

And damn, it was her kid's party.

"Thirty minutes," he conceded.


Back in the unmarked, JC hauled out his phone and tried again to reach the remaining Kaufman siblings. He'd gone to their homes earlier that morning. No one answered the door at Jessica and Jeremy's addresses. The guy living at Owen's listed address said, "Asshole moved out a month ago and stiffed me for the rent."

"Any idea where he went?"

"No clue. Can you collect the rent money when you see him?"

"Try small claims court."

Briefly, he wondered if Ryan had gotten hold of them late last night. If not, the article in the morning *Courier* should've had them contacting him, demanding answers.

Still no answer at any of the numbers the victim had in his contact list. After leaving messages—*please call me at your earliest opportunity*—he pulled over his laptop to start the never-ending paperwork for his earlier interviews.

He hesitated, then reached for his phone again. A quick scroll though his recent call list and a tap on a number connected him to Holly. "Hi."

He automatically turned his back on Madeline's house—and the investigation—before realizing what he'd done. He shifted and made a quick scan of the area. No visible threat. No fleeing suspect.

"Hi yourself." Holly's voice sparkled over the line. "I promise I'll only be at work a few more minutes."

"You're at work?" Irony poked at surprise.

"This rockcrawler event...it's nine million details. It's driving me nuts."

"Why are you planning that?"

"I'm not. At least I'm not supposed to be. But Walt calls me twenty times a day, which means I'm behind on everything else."

He laughed at her aggravated tone. "If it wasn't rockcrawlers, it'd be something else."

"And your point is?"

"I miss you." He put all the warmth he could muster into his voice.

"I miss you too. Good thing I'm seeing you tonight."

He heaved a sigh. "Yeah. About that."

"You're standing me up. Again." Her tone lost the happy vibe.

"You heard about that murder?" His free hand ground circles into his temple.

"And of course you were assigned to investigate."

"It's what I do."

"I know. I'm not going to argue with you about it. Go do what you have to do. But we have to figure out how to make this relationship work. It's hard to be in love with a guy you never see."

He swallowed hard. It was the first time she'd acknowledged she loved him. "I'll make it up to you."

"I don't need you to 'make it up to me.' I just need *you*." The last bit was a quiet sigh.

"I'll find a way."

After he disconnected, he cradled the phone as if it could keep his connection to Holly intact. He was going to lose her if he couldn't figure out a way to...to what? Manage his life? His job? He'd worked too hard to get her back into his life to let her go without a fight.

So figure out who killed Kaufman and get your own life back on track.

He pulled over the laptop. As he typed, he watched a parade of cars arrive at Madeline's house. An adult, usually a woman, popped out and rang the bell. He jotted down license plates in case he needed to talk to any of Madeline's friends later. While none outright stared at him, at least one must have noticed and considered him a pervert or predator. A call for service went out via the internal server. He quickly keyed in a response, dropping in his badge number— *Surveying a possible witness.*

The call cleared.

More often, a few minutes after they entered the house, the women re-emerged with a kid who was either bouncing off the walls or completely crashed. Finally the parade slowed to a trickle.

A neighbor stepped onto her front porch and stared at him.

He waited and sure enough, she edged closer. "If you don't leave, I'm calling the cops."

He rolled down his window and hung out his badge.

The self-righteous expression changed to one of fear. "Is everything okay?"

He climbed from the car. "May I ask you a few questions?"

The adrenaline that had carried the neighbor out the door seemed to fade. "What's going on?"

"Tell me about your neighbor." He nodded at the Larsson house.

Her hand flew to her throat. "Maddie? Is she okay? Asher hasn't been hassling her again has he?"

"Asher?" There was that name again.

"Her ex. Is that why you're here?"

"Tell me about Asher."

Her hand dropped into a crossed arm posture. "Asher is her deadbeat ex-husband. He shows up every now and then, usually drunk, and hits her up for money. And I do mean hit."

She was winding herself up again. "Her parents talked her into getting a protection order to keep him away from both her and Caden. The past few months have been better—he hasn't been as big of a problem. Well, not until last week." She waved a hand around, acknowledging she was babbling. "Maddie lets him see the boy." She shook her head. "Well, she lets Asher see Caden if he's sober. With all the ruckus for the boy's party, did one of the neighbors call you, thinking he might be over there?"

JC made a note to follow up on both the protection order and any call for violation of it. "You ever have any trouble with Madeline?"

"None. She's a nice girl. Works hard and that little boy is a sweetheart."

"She mostly works at night?"

"She works an odd schedule." The neighbor's arms still wrapped around her middle, but her facial expression was considering. "Usually her mother keeps her son. I've babysat a few times. Like I said, the child's a little boy, but he's no trouble. Then she goes to school during the day."

He pulled out the victim's photo. "Have you ever seen this man here?"

She studied the picture and shook her head." Who is he?"

"You sure?"

"Other than an occasional play date for Caden, Maddie doesn't have much of a social life."

JC took notes and pumped her for details, but the woman ran out of gossip after another round of complaints about the ex.

No new mommy-mobiles had arrived during his interview of the neighbor. JC thanked the woman and headed to Madeline's door. Once again, he rang the doorbell.

This time Madeline opened it with a little kid riding her hip.

He nodded at the boy. "Your son?"

"This is Caden." Her gaze dropped to her child and a proud mommy smile softened her face.

"Happy birthday."

The kid turned his face into his mother's shoulder.

Huh. His nieces and nephews didn't do that. Maybe the kid was shy. Or maybe he was spending too much time on the job and not enough with his family. He'd heard that compliant a lot lately. "May I come in?"

She hesitated, then swung the door wider. "Okay."

He followed her into a room still littered with wrapping paper. A pile of kid toys heaped the sofa and spilled onto the floor.

"Sorry about the mess." She glanced around. "The table?"

The round, wooden table looked freshly washed. The matching chairs were lined up in front of the peninsula that separated the small family room from the kitchen.

"Would you like a piece of birthday cake? Some coffee?"

"No thanks." He grabbed a chair, made sure it wasn't still wet and positioned it for her. He pulled over another chair and sat down on the opposite side of the table.

She clutched the kid in her lap. He wiggled, ready to get down, while shooting troubled glares at JC. "Who's he, Mommy?"

Apparently a strange man in the house was not a common event.

"He's a police officer, Caden."

The boy cut his eyes at JC, then snuggled closer to his mom. His lower lip quivered. "Are you mad at Daddy?"

She hugged his small body. "I'm sad your daddy didn't come to your party, but I don't think that's why the policeman's here."

That earned him another distrustful glance. "Why's he here?"

"He needs my help. He wants to ask me

questions."

The kid seemed to process and accept her story. "Can I go play?"

"You can pick *one* new toy or you can play in the back yard where I can see you. Your choice."

Caden jumped off her lap and ran to the toy pile. Within seconds he was making engine noises and ramming a firetruck into the carpet.

JC refocused on Madeline. He pulled the picture he'd gotten from Ryan and placed it on the table. "Do you know this man?"

She pulled the photo closer. "Sure, Daniel comes in the Tom Tom, the casino where I work, all the time."

"When was the last time you saw him?" JC slid out his notebook.

"This week has been such a blur between my car and getting ready for Caden's party." She rubbed her forehead. "It must have been Thursday since I had Friday off. Why? Has something happened? Is he okay?"

"Tell me about your relationship with him."

"Is there a reason you didn't answer my question? Is he okay?"

JC kept his expression neutral. "Daniel Kaufman was killed last night."

Her mouth sagged open. "Killed?" Her hand moved to her chest and her eyes clicked over to check out her son before she returned her attention to him. "What happened?"

"We're not sure, which is why I'm asking questions. Following his movements. He was at the casino on Thursday?"

She nodded. "I didn't see him leave, but he was

43

there at midnight when I took a break. I worked the poker tables after my first break and Daniel only plays blackjack. Did he wreck his car? Most nights he'll have a drink or two, but I never saw him drunk or unsteady on his feet. Our security guys are really good at watching for anybody who might be drunk. They call a cab instead of letting them leave in their own car. And the bartender will cut off anybody who looks like they're hammered."

She seemed to realize she was babbling because she abruptly closed her mouth.

JC waited a beat to see if she'd say more.

"Was he drinking on Thursday?"

"He had a drink." She tilted her head as if she were thinking. "He looked like maybe he didn't feel good or his insomnia was kicking in again."

"He had insomnia?" That could explain why the victim was out so late on Thursday. But who had he met or been with that night? Someone at or from the casino, or had the murder occurred later, after he left?

"He told me he sometimes has trouble sleeping." Madeline sighed. "That sweet old man. He's really dead?"

"Yes."

Her eyes filled with tears. She grabbed a paper napkin and dabbed at her eyes and blew her nose. "Sorry."

He made a few quick notes, giving her a moment to recover—but not so much time that she could organize a story behind those tears.

"You called him a 'sweet old man.' How well did you know him?"

Still clutching the napkin, her hands lifted from

the table in a vague gesture. "If I was dealing blackjack, he sat at my table. On slow nights we might chat a bit while he played. He seemed lonely, but he was fun. Funny."

"So he was a regular?"

"I guess you'd call him that." She shrugged.

This wasn't going to be one of those interviews where he simply had to be a good listener. Where the witness—or suspect—couldn't wait to tell their story. He was going to have to pull the information out, one question at a time. "How often did you see him?"

Her lips twitched and her gaze drifted for a moment. "He came in once or twice a week, during the week when it's quieter. I don't think I ever saw him on the weekends."

"Did you talk to him, other than when he played blackjack?"

"Sometimes he'd go to the snack bar with me during my break."

Was that allowed? Or were there rules against chatting up the gamblers? "What about Thursday? Did you talk to him then?"

She nodded. "Early in my shift. He came over to my blackjack table. But not during my midnight break."

"What did you talk about?"

"Well." Her gaze turned inward. "He talked about his kids a lot. He told me stories about being on the poker tour."

"There's a tour for that?"

"Uh, yeah." Her eyebrows rose in the universal *d'uh* expression and he again noticed how young she was. Young and pretty. Would she have caught an

45

old man's attention? Beyond the obvious appreciation of a pretty face.

"The tour's a big deal if you play cards. Daniel was really good when he was younger. He came back to the Tri-Cities after he retired so he could be with his kids and grandkids."

"He had family here? I thought you said he was lonely."

"I don't know." She twirled a strand of hair around a finger, noticed the smear of mud on her arm and swiped at it with the paper napkin. "It was more an impression than anything he said."

"How so?"

She dropped the messy paper napkin onto the table. A second later she rose, tossed it into the trashcan and checked on her son before returning to the table. "Maybe it was because he came in by himself and talked to me." She dropped into her seat, lips pursed as if she were thinking about it. Finally, she said, "If you have friends, you hang out with them. Even if you like coming to the casino to gamble or to watch a televised game, you're with them, at least part of the time. Daniel never did that."

He rubbed a hand across his jaw. "So the casino was a place to feel connected."

She cocked her head. "Could be. He chatted with other gamblers, but I didn't see him getting close to anybody."

How close did he get to her? Time to cut to the chase. "Did he give you money?"

A flush climbed her cheeks. Her arms crossed in a defensive move. "When you say it like that, you make it sound dirty." Her chin rose and anger flared in her eyes. "If he won, he left me a tip. Dealing cards is what I do. Tips are part of how I'm paid. Just like any other dealer at the casino."

"Mr. Kaufman never talked to you about his money?"

"He won a lot on the tour." She shrugged one shoulder, a quick jerk of her stiff posture. "I guess he still has part of it. He never made big bets when he played blackjack and it was why he wouldn't play poker at the Tom Tom. He said he didn't need to take the locals' money."

"He ever talk more specifically about it?"

She chewed her lip. "The only time I remember him mentioning his money was Thursday night. The last time he came in." Tears again welled in her eyes.

"And?"

She blinked away the tears. "I asked him about the black eye."

"Black eye?"

She tilted her head and studied him. "Didn't you see it? The bruise was still obvious on Thursday."

"Tell me about it."

Madeline recounted the argument between Daniel and his son about working and responsibility. "He said his son hit him when he wouldn't give him money. Who does that? Why do men have to hit when they're angry?"

Her hand moved to her left forearm and stroked the healing set of bruises. JC had noticed them earlier when he'd spotted the mud smear. The pattern made it fingerprints. Someone had grabbed her. Why? Who? The ex? Or the old man? Someone else? As casually as he could, he scanned her face and right arm. Along her jawline, another faint bruise was visible through her makeup.

Had the beatings been a common bond? Brought out a protective side of Kaufman? "You said 'the son' hit him. Do you know which son hit him?"

"I don't remember." Another shrug. "I was more upset about the hitting, than who did it. If I had to guess, I'd say his youngest one."

"Why do you say that?"

"Daniel mentioned—what's his name? Starts with an O. Oscar, Otis, Owen—that's it. Owen. Anyway, Daniel said... well... He complained about Owen a few times. Said he couldn't keep a job. He'd bailed him out before. I think he meant a financial jam, not like jail. I don't know what happened this time. Why Daniel said no or why Owen lost his temper."

JC scribbled notes. Ryan hadn't mentioned the argument or that there was friction between father and son. If the shiner was yellowing on Thursday, Daniel had it when he supposedly went to church with Ryan and Emily. Neither had mentioned the bruise. Whitewashing the family or covering up for the brother?

Damn, now he had to go talk to people at the church to see if the victim had been present Wednesday night and if so, had anyone noticed a bruise.

Another thought occurred to him as he considered the placement of the killing shot. Did the shooter know about the bruise? Was there enough light in the car to see it? Was the shot blowing out that part of the victim's face a coincidence or was the shooter covering up the earlier assault? Or was it part of the vindictive nature of the murder?

"I can't think of anything else."

JC jerked his attention back to the blonde. She tapped her fingers across the table as if she were itching to get up. "I can't tell you anything about Daniel outside the casino. I'm completely willing to help, but if that's it, I have a mess to clean up here."

"Did the vic—Mr. Kaufman—ever talk about his will?"

"His will to do what?"

Confusion twitched her eyebrows but she didn't shoot daggers at him. Jumping around usually kept suspects off their game, but maybe he needed to connect the dots for her. "His will. As in, last will and testament."

"Oh, you mean for when he died. Why would he talk to me about that? She raised a hand in a vague gesture. "He'd asked me about what I was going to school for, but we didn't talk about *personal* stuff. I mean, we didn't share life histories."

"Did he talk about your role in it?"

"In life? Uh, no?"

Was she playing obtuse or did she really not see the connection. "In his will."

Her eyebrows met in full confusion now. "Why would I be in his will? He isn't *my* dad."

"Sometimes people include non-family members in their bequests."

"Oh. Now I see where this is going." Color slowly climbed her cheeks. "Daniel warned me Owen might try to make trouble for me."

"In what way?"

"Owen made accusations about me being after Daniel's money." She sat ramrod straight, the flush betraying her anger. "Daniel thought Owen might spread some nasty rumors."

"And?" Ryan had made the same suggestion. Apparently he needed to move Owen up on his list of people to interview. If he could find the guy.

"And nothing. I work hard for my paycheck. I don't ask for or expect anything more. If that's why you're here, the door's right there." She rose, pointing toward her front door.

Caden looked up. He had the firetruck parked in front of the sofa. The ladder tilted into the cushion. "Mommy?"

Apparently the kid was attuned to his mother's emotional state. JC leaned back in his chair, as if he had all the time in the world. "I'm not accusing you of anything. I'm trying to find out what happened. Your perspective is as important as anything his son says."

Madeline crossed the room and stooped beside her kid. "What are you doing?"

"Putting out a fire." The tone—even in a four-year-old—added, *Isn't it obvious?*

"I see. Do you have helpers?"

Caden nodded. "Never go in alone."

"That's right. The firefighters said that was important." She turned back to JC. "You're still here."

Her tone with flat, her expression defiant.

He mostly had what he needed—for now. "One last question. Did you ever see Mr. Kaufman with a special poker chip?"

JC watched her silent struggle between wanting to hang onto her indignation and what was apparently a helpful nature.

Helpful won. With a huff, she picked up the kid and shifted him higher on her hip. "Daniel always

50

had his lucky chip with him. It was from his last tour championship game."

She confirmed Ryan's story about the chip's significance, but she talked about it too easily, especially given how pissed off she was. If she'd taken the chip, what would it be worth? Not to cash in, because the casino where the tour game was held most likely wouldn't honor it. But did it have value because it was part of that tournament? Did people collect poker junk the way they did for Nascar or Star Wars?

"Did you see it on Thursday?"

"Yes."

Thoughts and questions ran through JC's mind at a lightening pace. Why would she take the chip and not the wallet or at least the cash and credit cards? If she'd taken the chip, wouldn't she downplay its significance? Or deny seeing it on Thursday so that the vic could've left or lost it somewhere else?

A suspect's reactions were always telling. A sociopath could lie, but they couldn't fake emotion. So far, her reactions and answers cleared her, but he'd play it by the book. "Where were you Thursday night between midnight and 5 AM?"

"Excuse me?" Her mouth dropped open and an incredulous expression rounded her eyes.

"Where were you—"

"I heard that part. You think I did something to Daniel? Are you crazy?"

The kid clutched her shirt and howled.

She patted his back and did that rocking thing women did with crying kids.

"It's a routine question. If you have an alibi, I can mark you off the list and focus on the people who

51

might have harmed him."

"I worked until 3:00 AM." Anger snapped blue sparks in her eyes. "It'll be on a dozen security videos. From 3:15 to 4:00 AM, I was in the parking lot with a car that wouldn't start. And before you ask, Frank Phalen, our security chief, was there and so was the tow truck driver who gave me a time-stamped receipt."

"Frank Phalen?" A muscle twitched in his jaw as he struggled to keep his tone level. Great. Just what he needed. Another woman mixed up with Phalen. JC had enough trouble keeping the former cop out of his own girlfriend's life.

"Frank gave me a ride to my parents' house after the tow truck left."

Easy enough to confirm. Every angle had to be checked at this stage of an investigation, but he had a feeling her alibi would be solid. JC pocketed his notebook.

She trailed him to the door, still comforting her son.

The boy's tears bugged him. He felt like a jerk for ruining the kid's birthday. And as much as he usually managed to avoid it, he'd allowed Ryan—and the firefighters—to color his initial impression of Madeline.

The kid's tears didn't bother him nearly as much as her revelation about Phalen's involvement in his investigation and her life.

With each step, his conscience battled procedure. Phalen. Shit. The asshole disgraced the uniform, made JC's girlfriend's life miserable, and had nearly gotten Holly killed.

He reached for the door handle.

If the guy was hanging around Madeline...

His fingers cramped around the cold metal.

Professionalism be damned. He had to warn her.

He turned around. "Keep your distance from Frank Phalen. He's trouble."

# CHAPTER SIX

*Late Saturday afternoon*

JC Dimitrak rolled to a stop beside the Pasco fire station. Still unable to reach the other Kaufman siblings, he'd talked to several of the victim's neighbors after leaving Madeline's home. *"We rarely see his children and the grandchildren over there,"* they'd stated.

Owen was the exception. "Now Owen, he's there all the time. Not helping out, you know. Just lying around. There's one in every family."

That last bit had been accompanied by rueful headshakes. "Failure to launch."

Both neighbors had told him about a fierce argument between father and son the week before the victim's death. While they hadn't seen a physical battle, the timing was consistent with the bruising Madeline described.

The fire station's big garage door was open and the fire engine was back in its bay. Several of the firefighters were visible inside the station. Others were on a different rig, washing it down. A guy JC knew, Don Taber, crouched over a dismantled piece of equipment.

"Dimitrak. How's it hanging?" Taber stepped

away from the gear, picked up a shop rag and wiped his hands. "Thought I saw you when we were packing up over at Maddie's house."

JC crossed his arms and slid an easy grin over his face. "I gotta ask. What would you have done if there was a fire?"

"We'd have rolled." Taber tossed the rag onto the equipment cart.

"With a dozen kids hanging on?"

"Nah. We'd shake them off first." Taber widened his stance. Lines on his face deepened as he smiled. "Her kid, Caden. We might've let him ride along. Had to arm wrestle him for my helmet."

"Yeah, it's your gear, not you." He remembered the kid's reaction to a police officer in the house. Guess firefighters didn't bust his daddy for abuse.

"Maybe you shoulda worn your uniform. What were you doing there, anyway?"

With easy practice, JC ignored the question. "Who's dating Madeline? Did she call or did one of you hose-draggers volunteer a full turnout at her house?"

"Whoa, what a minute. This is official?"

"Gotta ask a few questions. I need to understand why you were there."

"Phalen asked us to swing by." Taber shrugged. "The guy's done us a few favors. It was kinda fun."

"Frank Phalen?" JC stifled the wince. Was the guy going to be a pain in his ass for the rest of his life? Why did Phalen have to move to the Tri-Cities from Seattle? The guy swore it wasn't because he was still stalking Holly.

Right.

That wasn't why he kept tripping over the loser.

"Security at the Tom Tom casinos. You know him?"

"What kind of favors?" JC kept the question neutral, even as his mind imagined the kind of shit the former cop had arranged.

"He's let us use that back room. Guys' night. Held a few poker parties. Texas Hold 'Em." Taber lifted a shoulder in a dismissive shrug.

"Disgraced himself as law enforcement so now he wants to be a fireman? Thought your standards were higher than that." The words were out before he thought better of it.

Taber stiffened. "Back up. You clearly have a problem with the guy. Leave me out of it." He turned, slammed the door on one of the engine's side compartments, and grabbed a wrench off the equipment cart. "If you have *official* questions, talk to the captain."

JC bit off a harsh response. Taber was right. He was letting his feelings about Phalen interfere with his job.

JC approached the Tom Tom Two, aware he was gearing up for a confrontation. He had to put his personal issues with Frank Phalen aside.

The stalking. Holly's nightmares. Yeah. He'd put all that right out of his mind when he questioned the guy about a suspect's alibi.

His hands tightened on the steering wheel. Damn but he hated Phalen. The abuse of power. The misery he'd caused. The asshole was the polar opposite of everything he believed about his job and his life.

He sat in the parked car and stared at the casino while taking long slow breaths. His fingers flexed, pushing away the tension and anger. *Get it together.*

He would make a mess of this case if he let Phalen color his thinking. Let him get inside his head and distract him.

Enough.

Time for a full stop/reset on his attitude and the investigation. He knew how to do his job.

So do it.

Five minutes later, he tugged open the entrance door, stepped into the casino, and automatically scanned the interior. The place looked nicer than he expected given what he'd seen of the original Tom Tom. Someone who knew what they were doing had planned the layout and security details. A barred window—the cashier—centered the right hand wall. Several doorways punctuated the other walls of the entryway. Guards were stationed near the entrances, conveniently close enough to the cashier window to discourage a player from trying something stupid, while also providing coverage for the various gaming areas. Peering through the openings, JC could see the bar, a card room and the long rows of slot machines.

The crowd in the bar was focused on the big screen TVs. Saturday afternoon. College football was playing. The fans were noisy but not rowdy. JC couldn't remember which teams U Dub or WaZoo were playing that weekend.

Yet another sign he spent too much time on the job.

He moved on to the slots. People stood or sat on stools before machines that clanged with bells and flashed sufficient lights to induce a seizure. He recognized the alert people in the room, the ones who were likely security, by their posture.

Peering into the card room, Madeline's blonde hair caught his attention. She worked a blackjack table near the middle of the room. Her hands moved constantly, dealing cards, clearing chips and discarded hands, paying out occasionally. She smiled at the players, mouthing the occasional word, but didn't waste time chatting them up. Sensing movement behind him, JC turned to discover one of the security guards closing on him.

"Help you with something?"

JC flipped open his badge case. "I'm looking for your security chief, Frank Phalen."

"Mr. Phalen is in the sports bar." The guard, a stocky Hispanic guy, nodded toward the noisy room.

"Is there an office or quiet spot? I need to talk with him."

"The offices are back there." He pointed at an unmarked door beyond the cashier. "That's a restricted area. I'll ask Mr. Phalen to step out. He'll have to escort you."

"Great." Keep it civil. Don't let Phalen get under your skin.

The guard signaled one of his counterparts, who shifted position in response to Guard One's departure. JC wondered if Phalen had inherited the security setup or implemented it. Either way, he grudgingly admitted the coverage was good.

A minute later Guard One returned, trailing Frank Phalen. The cowboy hat shaded Phalen's features, but JC caught the momentary falter in his gait. The guard peeled away and Phalen continued across the entry hall.

"You wanted to see me?" The tone was cool. Polite.

"I'm investigating the murder of one of your patrons. This casino was his last known location. I'd like to review your security footage for Thursday night."

Phalen nodded, one sharp dip of his chin. "This way."

He led the way to the unmarked door, pulled out a badge and scanned the lock open. A modern office lay beyond the closed door. Several cubicles held empty desks. A middle-aged woman typed at a computer in another. She glanced up as the men approached, scanning past Phalen to give JC a considering inspection. JC nodded at her as they passed.

Phalen's office was against the back wall, the end unit in a set of three. He tossed the cowboy hat onto a file cabinet, then dropped into the desk chair without a word and clicked around on the computer keys. "What time on Thursday?"

"The victim was reported here from roughly eleven PM to midnight, so bracket an hour on either end."

Phalen clicked more keys, grabbed a box of CDs, and slapped one into the computer drive. "Those four hours, all cameras."

The first moments of file copying were silent. JC shifted his weight and leaned against the doorframe. "I also need a second time period."

Phalen looked up. His face was perfectly still but the tension in his shoulders matched the antagonism in his eyes. JC figured the guy reciprocated his feelings. Maybe hated him more since JC was with the woman Phalen had wanted.

"When and who?" The security chief flexed his fingers over the keyboard.

"Closing time. One of your employees claims she had car trouble."

For a long moment Phalen stared at him. "Madeline Larsson. Her car wouldn't start. I called the tow truck. I'm sure my word isn't good enough for you." He turned back to the computer. "You want her entire shift or just the parking lot."

JC thought about it. He might not get a second shot at the files. The few minutes he'd watched her tonight said she didn't flirt with the players. Was that consistent behavior or concern she might now be under observation? "Go ahead with the full shift. The parking lot too."

Phalen's fingers tapped through the keys. He grabbed another CD, removed the first one and labeled it while the second batch of files transferred. He tapped more keys, then spun the monitor toward JC. The oversized screen split into multiple windows. On all of them, the young blonde card dealer, carrying a purse and package, walked toward a small cluster of cars. The time stamp in the corner moved constantly, closing in on 03:15 AM. "I'm running it at double time."

The ME estimated a window of midnight to five AM for the victim's death. The security feeds were going to clear his suspect for over half of that time. "Not many people on the back shift."

"That time of night, most people play the slots. The bar's open, but we only have a couple of dealers in-house."

On the screen, the girl reached her car and apparently tried to start it. One angle showed her pounding on the steering wheel—yeah, that would really help—before despair slumped her in the driver's seat. A moment later, she snapped to attention and Frank entered the field of view.

They watched in silence.

"Awful convenient you were here that night."

A beat passed. "We had an incident earlier that night with card counters. I was finishing my paperwork when I noticed her still sitting in the car."

The video stream showed Phalen trying to start the car, talking on the phone, and then the two waiting for the tow truck. JC managed not to ask about the cozy conversation in the front seat of her car. The video was blowing away Madeline's opportunity to meet Kaufman, shoot him, get home—without an operating car—and set up her kid's birthday party.

"And you just jumped at the chance to help her." JC cursed himself for letting the words out of his mouth. But damn. His prime—only—suspect had a really good alibi. And Frank Fucking Phalen provided it.

"She's an employee. It's my parking lot. The casino could be liable if she ran into trouble."

"Of course." JC wrestled his animosity under control. "Wonder why she didn't call a friend or family member? Or a cab?"

"Three in the morning probably had something to do with it." Phalen's tone was dry. "She asked for the phone number of a cab when the tow truck showed up."

"Do you remember which company?" Like there

were so many in the Tri-Cities.

"I gave her a lift."

Phalen was tense, like he expected JC to make another snide remark.

"Where?" Treat Phalen like any other alibi witness.

"I took her to her parents'. It was about four AM. She said good night and went inside. Alone."

"She could've left," JC mused. The video went blank after Phalen drove away from the casino lot with the girl in his Jeep.

"She's a nice woman." Phalen handed over the labeled discs, then rose, reaching for his hat. "I don't mind helping someone out."

"That seems to be her specialty." JC tapped the discs against his thigh. "Getting men to help her." The firefighters. Phalen. Had Daniel Kaufman? Was that why he was dead?

"She's never asked me for a thing." Phalen jammed his cowboy hat onto his head and stepped toward the door. "I have work to do."

JC walked away from the security office, rerunning the timetable in his head. It was a really narrow window but with help, Madeline still could've killed Daniel Kaufman.

The question became, who would've helped her?

Then again...He dropped the discs into his pocket and slid out his notebook. A quick flip through his notes produced a phone number.

"Hello?" The woman's voice was pleasant and mellow.

He introduced himself. "I'm investigating the death of a friend of your daughter's and would like to clear her and move on to other people."

"The death?" Mrs. Larsson gasped. "Are you referring to that man who was murdered?"

"Yes ma'am."

"Goodness, surely you don't think Maddie had anything to do with that?"

"Ma'am, I understand Madeline was at your home Friday morning?" He turned to a clean page and noted the time and date of the call.

"Yes. Yes."

He could visualize her startled blink and re-focus on his question.

"Maddie was asleep on the couch when I came downstairs. I hated to wake her since she got in so late."

"What time was that?"

"That I woke her or that she came in?" Her tone had cooled considerably.

"Both."

"She came in shortly after four and let us know she wasn't a burglar. I woke her about seven."

Running on three hours sleep. Sounded like his job.

"One last question. What was she wearing when you woke her?"

"Her clothes from the casino. Why?"

"Thank you, Mrs. Larsson. You've given me what I needed to confirm her alibi."

Which meant he had to come up with new suspects.

# CHAPTER SEVEN

*Sunday, early afternoon*

Jessica Hensley's home was a near duplicate of her brother Ryan's house. New subdivision in north Pasco. Pale yellow siding, a touch of glue-on rock at the entrance, a bit of Northwest Craftsman style, and a concrete path cutting a straight line through a green grass front yard. JC parked behind the vehicles in the driveway, wondering if the couple had guests or if the garages were full of boxes. He made a note of the license plates for the Suburban and a Dodge Ram pickup.

He'd stopped by the Kaufman's church earlier that morning and caught the pastor after services ended. She couldn't remember if Daniel Kaufman or his kids had attended the previous Wednesday, but confirmed they usually did. She'd pointed out a few people in the departing congregation who were regulars. None of them could say for sure whether the family had been at the church's mid-week service.

Had Ryan lied, or in the stress of the moment had he simply mixed up his dates? Offered the usual routine? JC had a trained memory for detail. Ryan had said, "He *goes* to church with us" rather than, "He *went* to church with us."

It was a minor detail—maybe not even relevant to the murder timeline—but it bugged him. There had to be a way to confirm it one way or the other. More neighbor interviews. More time at the church.

Unless he could find the killer quickly, the investigation would settle into a long grind. Persistence and following the thinnest threads of leads were part of the job. JC suspected Ryan was trying to make the family look good. It happened a lot with the families of murder victims. But so far the window dressing seemed unnecessary. Implying there were things to hide—and every family had them—made him curious about what the Kaufman family didn't want him to see.

Where were the cracks in this family's facade?

Two minutes later, JC was sitting in a comfortable, middle class family room studying a female version of Ryan Kaufman. Like her brother, Jessica looked younger than her twenty-nine years. Casually dressed in sweat pants and a fleece shirt, Jessica had scraped her blonde hair into a ponytail but she still wore full, I-went-to-church makeup. With her wide cheeks and bright blue eyes, she was pretty in a wholesome mommy way.

Her husband, Christopher, sat beside her. About five foot, eleven, JC put Christopher's weight pushing past two hundred pounds. A lot of defined muscle covered his frame but JC attributed at least ten of those pounds to the half-full beer sitting beside the recliner in front of the muted television. Periodically Christopher's gaze drifted to his abandoned football game. Apparently Daniel's death hadn't been a world rocker for him.

"Have you found the person who killed my

father?" Jessica leaned forward, her fingers clenched together in her lap.

Damn those TV cop shows. Real crimes weren't solved in thirty minutes. "We're investigating."

"What does that mean?"

"It means we're interviewing everyone who might know about the victim or the crime, and gathering forensic evidence." JC pulled his notebook from his pocket and opened it to a fresh page.

Jessica sat up straighter. "But I thought that tramp at the casino, the Tom Tom, shot him."

He considered the fresh-faced young mother he'd met the previous day. Yeah, he'd gone in with questions about Madeline's involvement, but "tramp" wasn't the first word he'd use to describe her. "Why do you say that?"

"Ryan, Owen..." Jessica trailed off, as if realizing she had no concrete evidence to support her accusation.

As if that ever stopped anyone.

JC noticed she didn't include Jeremy, the third brother in her list of accusers. Why the exclusion? He'd finally gotten hold of Jeremy. The guy worked the night shift and turned off his cell during the day while he slept. They'd arranged to meet later that evening. "What did your brothers tell you?"

Jessica dropped her gaze and twisted the rings on her fingers. "Dad made a lot of money on the poker tour. He won ten million dollars in that last tournament. And that wasn't his only win. Ryan and Owen said that girl"—an upgrade from tramp—"was after his money."

They make that kind of money playing poker? Maybe he should brush off his card skills.

Nah.

But seriously? Ten million? Or did four million come off the top for taxes? When the payoff amount included "million," did it matter?

"Did they tell you why they suspected her?" he asked.

She lifted one shoulder in a half shrug. "Dad talked about her. How tough she had it. Single mother. Lousy ex. Blah, blah, blah. It sounded like a sob story. A way to soften him up. Like she wanted to worm her way in."

"Did your father give her money?"

Jessica squirmed a little. Christopher cast another longing look at the television. "Dad played cards at that casino all the time. He's so generous, I know he tipped her every time he went there."

"Wouldn't he do that for any of the dealers?"

Blotches of pink colored Jessica's neck and cheeks. "I guess."

"So you aren't aware that he specifically gave her money?"

She hesitated, glanced sideways at her husband who offered no answer. Finally Jessica shook her head. The ponytail flipped across her shoulders, making her look even younger.

"Is there anyone else"—other than four kids who potentially would inherit north of a million each—"who might've had a disagreement with your father?"

Another headshake from Jessica. "I don't think Dad saw many people besides us, his family. Other than the people at the casino, I mean."

"Did he mention other people from the casino?"

"I can't think of anybody." She turned to her

husband. "Chris, you talked to Dad about cards. Did he mention anybody?"

"Nope." He slid an arm around Jessica. "Daniel was an easy-going guy. He always had a string of friends. With his personality, he attracted people but it wasn't the same ones twice."

Was "easy-going" consistent with savvy enough to play poker at the highest levels? More smokescreen or did they really not know the victim at all? "So it's possible the person who attacked him was a new acquaintance?"

Christopher shrugged. "No idea. I'm just saying he didn't have many close friends other than his kids."

JC's attention shifted back to Jessica. "When did you last see your father?"

Her blush deepened.

He loved fair complexions. The pale skin made it so much easier to see the guilt painted across a blonde's face. "He came over at Halloween. He wanted to see the kids' costumes. There are a lot more kids in our neighborhood. He had a great time handing out candy to the Trick-or-Treaters." That last bit came out with a touch of defensiveness—and a bit of defiance.

"A generous nature." JC noted the date.

"He is. Was." Tears filled Jessica's blue eyes.

JC tapped his pen against the notebook. "Halloween was what? The week before the murder?"

If possible, the blush deepened.

"We all led busy lives." Christopher rejoined the conversation.

"Honey." Jessica blinked back her tears and

placed a quelling hand on his arm.

Too busy for Daddy until it was time to collect the cash? JC stamped on the cynical observation.

"We usually got together once a week, had him over for dinner, invited him to events at the kids' schools. He got together with my brothers on a regular basis too."

"Did you see him the week before he was killed?"

She let out a deep sigh. "No. I'll regret that for the rest of my life."

"Why not?"

"The kids had practice for their school play on Tuesday. That's the day he usually came over for dinner. He didn't want to go."

JC flipped back a page in his notebook, as if he were searching for a comment. "You said he went to events at the children's schools."

"Events. Not rehearsal."

"What are you saying?" Christopher demanded. "That we had something to do with his death?"

*Did you?* "Since you didn't see your father that week, were you aware he'd argued with his son?"

Christopher subsided and Jessica shot another glance at her husband. "Which of my brothers did he argue with?" The innocence level was over the top.

"So you're saying you weren't aware of an argument."

She froze for a second. He figured she was generally an honest person and wondered if her husband or her brothers had told her to lie about the argument and resulting black eye.

"Ryan might've mentioned it when we saw him at church on Wednesday." She twisted the ring on

CATHY PERKINS

her right hand.

"Your dad usually go to church with you?" JC tamped down the spike of interest.

"We all go on Sundays. The preacher had a lovely sermon this morning. Our congregation is like an extended family. Everyone is in shock over Dad's death and her words were so uplifting."

JC remembered the overflowing house and endless casseroles when his grandfather died, an outpouring he'd seen with other victims' families. He'd noticed the sympathy cards, flowers, and a new potted plant when he entered the Hensley's house. "Are there church services during the week? Do you attend those?"

"We have Wednesday services. Sometimes Dad comes, but not last week."

*Not at church*, JC jotted in his notebook. He'd eventually find someone at that church who could confirm it, but why the lie? And who was lying? Ryan or Jessica? Given Jessica's inability to hide any emotion, he was betting on Ryan.

JC turned back to Christopher. "You work at the airport, right?"

"Horizon," he confirmed.

Alaska Airlines' puddle jumper affiliate, JC translated. "You're familiar with the area near the airport then."

Christopher tensed as if sensing a trap. "Yeah."

"Most people take 20th Avenue straight into the airport."

The guy dipped his chin, a quick acknowledgement.

"You'd be aware that Argent turns off right before the airport and runs over to 4th."

70

"So? Lots of people take that road."

Actually they didn't. The area was sparsely populated and other than a gas station, the businesses didn't generate commercial traffic. "The businesses over on 4th near the rail yard. What time are they usually open?"

Christopher heaved an oversized shrug. "Don't know. Never paid that much attention."

The guy didn't react to the mention of 4th Avenue—the place Daniel's car and body had been found—but his tension was disproportionate to the question. JC rubbed his temple as if he were thinking. "Most of the Horizon flights leave early in the morning. Heading out to catch up with longer flights out of Seattle and Denver."

"Yeah."

"What time do you go to work?"

"What?" Christopher leaned forward, a touch of aggression in his posture.

"The first flight is when? 05:30? 06:00?"

"5:50."

"So you get to work about 04:00? 04:30?"

"My shift starts at 4:30."

"Is that your usual work schedule?" JC make a quick notation.

"I like the early shift. I'm here when the kids get home from school. I coach their sport teams, something I couldn't do if I worked nine to five somewhere else."

"Must be great for your kids—and you too, Jessica—that you can work that schedule." JC flashed a glance at Jessica. She twisted her fingers together while watching her husband. As if she sensed his scrutiny, she turned, met his eyes for a moment, then looked away.

Interesting.

He refocused on Christopher. "Friday morning, the third, you got to work at the regular time?"

The guy sat back and crossed his arms. "I don't remember what time I clocked in."

Easy enough to find out. A quick phone warrant would pave the way. "How did you get to the airport that morning?"

Christopher gave him a hard stare. His jaw muscle bunched and flexed. "Straight up 20th."

JC made a note to check the traffic and security cameras in the area. Christopher would inherit right along with Jessica. A million reasons to kill the old man.

"So nothing out of the ordinary that morning?"

He saw the trickle of hesitation in the guy's eyes. "Nope."

*Okay.* A flicker of interest sparked. With deliberate indifference he turned to Jessica. This was just the first of many interviews he'd conduct with this pair. He needed more leverage—some evidence—before he tried to find out what was behind Christopher's hesitation. "What about you, Jessica? You get up when Christopher leaves for work?"

"God, no." She blinked. "I mean, he gets up at four. In the morning. Even in the summer, it's still dark at that hour. I learned to sleep through that a long time ago. I need those two hours of sleep before getting the kids up, dressed, fed and to school."

Christopher's alibi for the hours before 04:30 just vanished. JC caught the guy's resigned sigh.

# CHAPTER EIGHT

*Sunday afternoon*

"I can't believe they brought a firetruck to your house." Lauren followed Maddie out of the Tom Tom's dealer room.

"The truck, the crew." Maddie waved her hands around. "Caden was over the moon. He's talked about it non-stop. I swear, I had to go five miles out of my way when I took him to Mom's today just so we wouldn't drive past a fire station."

"So..." Lauren nudged her shoulder. "Were any of the firemen cute?"

She gave Lauren her best are-you-out-of-your-mind expression. "I had a dozen four-year-olds running me ragged. Like I had time to look?"

"Girl, you aren't dead. You're single. You oughta be looking."

She considered the detective who'd come to her house. He was cute.

Who was she kidding? He was hot, but he thought she was either a murderer or a bimbo who'd go after a sweet old man like Daniel for money.

Which totally pissed her off.

Yeah, nothing happening there. Not that he'd encouraged anything.

She elbowed Lauren. "So according to you, I'm looking for a firefighter with a soft spot for four-year-olds."

"You mean a fireman with a hard-on for twenty-something single moms."

"Can we make this not about sex?"

"What's wrong with sex?"

"You!" The snarling word boomed across the lobby.

The women snapped their attention toward the Tom Tom's sports bar. A man Maddie had never seen before stood at the entrance.

"You little bitch." He stormed out of the bar.

Both women took an instinctive step back. Behind the angry man, heads turned, taking in the scene.

"Who's he?" Lauren whispered.

"I'm not sure." The guy had Daniel's eyes. The sinking feeling in her stomach said she was about to meet one of Daniel's sons. He'd warned her they might cause trouble. She planted her feet and raised her chin. Daniel's kids could make all the noise they wanted but she hadn't done anything wrong. No more cowering when a guy got aggressive. Even that detective had backed down on Saturday when she stood up for herself. Not that the cop had been anywhere near this mean.

Or threatening.

Or...

Her gaze darted past the bar. Where were the security guys?

"You killed my father."

Maddie didn't know if the guy's red eyes and nose were the result of rage, grief, or beer.

74

"WTF?" Lauren stepped behind Maddie.

"I did not." Maddie held her ground. "You're Owen, aren't you?"

The loser kid Daniel had complained about.

Other guys spilled out of the bar.

"Damn straight. I'm Daniel's son. I'm gonna make you pay for what you did."

"I didn't do anything." Her gaze clicked over to the spectators. Would one of them jump in if security didn't show up?

"You were after his money." Owen's hands closed into fists as he stomped closer.

Like you weren't? "I never asked Daniel for anything." Her heart was in overdrive and her hands shook, but her voice sounded strong.

One beefy hand clenched, he cocked his right arm. "I oughta beat the shit out of you. You got him to change his will. It's your fault he's dead. You think you're gonna get away with it?"

Fear danced a jig in her stomach but her feet didn't move.

"Yo dude. Take it down a notch." One of the guys from the bar moved closer.

Lauren tugged at her shoulder. "This guy's nuts. Run."

She shook her head, not sure if she could make words come out her mouth.

Owen reached out, as if he planned to grab her arm or her shirt and start pounding—a move she'd seen Asher make too many times. Fighting the urge to cringe, she threw out her hands to fend him off. "Don't!"

Frank Phalen stepped in front of her. "Stop. Right there."

The guy rocked his fist and leaned in. "Get out of my way, asshole."

"You will not hurt one of my employees." Frank's lethal tone added weight to the words. "You will not hit anyone inside or outside this casino."

"Thank God," slipped out on a sigh of relief. Twice this week, Frank had bailed her out without making her feel incompetent.

"I didn't start it. She did." Owen's hand uncurled into a finger poked at Maddie. He retightened it into a clenched, cocked fist. "If you hired her, you're in it as deep as she is."

Owen swung at Frank, who caught the guy's wrist, pivoted and somehow the guy's arm was twisted behind his back.

"Holy crap." Lauren shrieked.

"Fuck off," Owen yelled and twisted, trying to free his arm.

Frank must have applied more pressure because Owen bellowed more curses and bent nearly double. Another security guard emerged from the crowd. He grabbed the crazy guy's shoulder and hauled him upright.

Frank turned to her. His hand rose toward her shoulder, but he didn't touch her. "Are you okay? Did he hurt you?"

Holy smokes. Not only did Frank have her back and take care of the situation, he cared about how she was reacting.

He realized she was more than a little out of her element.

Before Maddie could figure out how to make her mouth work, another man stepped out of the crowd. The detective who'd questioned her strode over to

Frank and slapped handcuffs onto Owen. "Good work, Phalen."

Maddie watched the detective's eyes as he ground out the words. Her gaze clicked over the Frank, who looked just as stony-faced as the cop. What on earth was going on between those two? Not that she really cared. All she cared about was she'd stood up for herself and the combination of Frank and Detective Dimitrak—that was his name—had crazy Owen headed toward the security office.

Owen writhed in a futile attempt to escape the handcuffs and Frank's grip. "What are you doing here? You can't follow me around, harassing me." His fury was aimed at the detective this time. "Why am I in cuffs and she's running around free?"

"You threatened a woman and took a swing at security." Detective Dimitrak's voice was cool.

"She robbed and killed my father." Owen twisted toward Maddie, his face distorted with rage. "This isn't over, bitch." Spit flew from his mouth. "You aren't getting away with it."

"Whoa," Lauren breathed. "You better watch your back, girl."

Maddie could only nod. Her face and chest flashed burning and freezing warnings as Owen's threats pingponged through her head.

The security guard hauled Owen toward the office corridor. Just before the group disappeared through the doorway, Detective Dimitrak spun toward her and jabbed a finger. "Don't leave."

Maddie stood rooted to the spot. What did that mean? Don't leave the lobby? The casino? Town?

What could he possibly think she'd done this time?

Thirty minutes later, the floor boss appeared beside Maddie's table. She'd been dealing like a mad woman, desperately avoiding thinking about Owen's threat. With all the commotion outside the bar, every seat at her table was taken and several people stood behind them, watching every move she made. She couldn't remember walking back to her station, transitioning the chips and shoe, and she had no idea if she'd calculated bets and payoffs correctly. She was pretty sure she'd dodged any questions about Owen's accusation, if only because she couldn't string together three words in a coherent sentence.

She flinched when the replacement dealer tapped her shoulder. With the eye in the sky undoubtedly tracking every move she made, it was inevitable the pit boss would either fire her or relieve her.

"You're needed at the security office," the floor boss said. "Angela's relieving you."

Of course security wanted to talk to her about what happened. Hopefully, that discussion would only be about Owen, and her job wasn't in jeopardy. She gave the floor boss a tight smile. Clearing her hands, showing them front and back, she stepped away to the right.

Angela immediately transitioned in. "You having a good night?" she asked the assembled players. "Let's gamble."

The guard took Maddie's arm, but it was a loose hold. More an "I'm being polite and guiding you" rather than, "I'm hauling you out of here." People still stared, but Maddie was too concerned about what lay on the other side of the security door to

78

worry about what the gamblers might think.

After a silent walk, the guard opened the office door. Maddie stepped inside and blinked. Detective Dimitrak sat at the desk rather than Frank.

Well, at least it wasn't HR or a management person, prepared to fire her.

Then again, getting arrested wasn't an improvement.

Before she could say a word, the detective said, "Please. Sit down."

It was a nice request rather than an order. She dropped into the chair beside the desk and stared at him. He looked grim and as if he could use more than a couple hours of sleep.

He splayed the fingers of his right hand against the desk and propped his chin on his other fist. His expression softened as he studied her. "Are you okay?"

If his concern wasn't genuine, then he was a damn fine actor. She nodded. She was scared. Worried about her job. Freaked out by the past few days, but basically okay. She was still breathing.

"Do you want to press charges against Owen Kaufman?"

"He didn't hit me. And I don't think he planned it or meant to hit anyone. He'd been drinking..." She stopped and shook her head. All of that was irrelevant. "Won't it be worse the next time I see him if he goes to jail because of me?"

It was one of the challenges she'd faced with Asher before she divorced him.

After she divorced him too. Her standing up to him just made him angrier and more likely to lash out.

Why, why, why had Asher started drinking again?

She severed the line of thought. Focus. Here. Now. Owen.

The detective sighed and jotted in the notebook that seemed to be an extension of him. "I figured you'd say that."

"What? That I wouldn't press charges?" Or that I'd excuse Owen's behavior? With a jolt, she realized that was exactly what she was doing. She'd done it with Asher. She'd let him wiggle out of responsibility for his actions by blaming...fill in the blank. Booze. A boss. A customer. Always someone or something else.

"Generally, with a perpetrator who isn't a habitual offender, jail gives him a chance to cool off. Given how volatile this Kaufman guy is, it's a good thing he's going to jail for attacking the security guard. It keeps him where he can't lash out and buys us some time to finish our investigation."

"You can lock people up when they haven't been convicted of a crime?" She stared at the cop, stunned.

Dimitrak shifted in his chair, wariness written across his expression. "With reasonable cause, we can detain people until they're charged."

Maddie's lips twisted into a half frown. She didn't want Owen back in the casino making trouble, but it seemed wrong.

Stop making excuses for him. Owen—and Asher—had to grow up and accept responsibility for their actions.

"If the judge declines to hold Kaufman after he's charged, do you and your son have somewhere else you can stay for a few days?" The detective slipped his notebook into his jacket pocket.

"Owen knows where I live?" Both her eyebrows and her voice shot skyward.

"With the internet, it isn't hard to find out."

"We could stay with my parents." She jammed fingers into her hair, as if her hands could keep her head from exploding. "What if he shows up there?"

She hadn't done anything wrong. Why were she and Caden at risk? Why were her parents?

"I was thinking more along the lines of a hotel or, even better, getting out of town for a few days."

"I can't miss work or school. A hotel isn't in the budget." Her hands dropped into her lap. Could this week get any worse?

"I won't name you specifically in the complaint to the judge. We'll try to hold Kaufman as long as we can."

"So it's up to the judge."

"Initially. Do you want to request a restraining order? Kaufman made a threat, tried to assault you. Threatened to come at you again."

She hesitated, then nodded. This was about Owen and his behavior, not anything she'd done. She needed to nip off the guilty feelings right now.

Caden—not Owen and not Asher—was her first priority.

She'd do whatever it took to keep her son safe.

# CHAPTER NINE

JC caught the call for service at the Tom Tom casino as he left Jessica and Christopher's home. Rather than pull in one of the uniforms when he was right up the road from the place, JC had responded. The last thing he'd expected to find was Owen Kaufman threatening Madeline Larsson.

Poor kid. He rose from the borrowed desk in the casino's security section and pocketed his phone and notebook. She'd had a rough week.

Yeah, he'd wondered when Ryan, Jessica and Owen painted her ugly enough to land her at the top of the suspect list. It had taken only a few minutes of talking to her to see she was a good kid.

He picked up the digital recording of Kaufman charging at Madeline and attacking the security chief. Taking a swing at Phalen was beyond dumb, but Owen didn't seem to think much through. Daniel Kaufman's murder might have been the result of a similar explosive emotional outburst. A lack of self-control had led Owen to hit his father last week and attack Madeline and Phalen today.

It made Owen stupid. It didn't make him a murderer.

And the killer seemed a lot more organized.

If Owen did it, he was either putting on a damn good show now or else he'd had help covering it up.

Blaming Madeline would be consistent transference behavior. Someone else made them do…whatever. Was the reason for his actions—up to and including the actual crime.

Either way, a uniformed officer was transporting Owen Kaufman to jail.

JC left the casino security office, nodded to a couple of the guys who'd helped him with Owen and the video recordings, and headed for his car.

He needed the county's forensic people to wrap up their analysis of the murder scene. He already had the preliminary reports on the fingerprints. The problem was, even if one of the kids was the killer, there would be a logical reason for their prints and other trace evidence to be all over their Dad's car. A defense attorney would shred the case if that was all he had.

He needed specifics that tied one of the siblings to the crime.

Uniformed officers were searching shrubbery and trashcans near the business where the victim and his car were found. So far, they hadn't located the gun or any other evidence they could tie to the homicide. If the killer tossed everything into the Columbia River, they might never find it.

The forensic team had moved the victim's vehicle to the lab. They'd scheduled a briefing for first thing Monday morning. Hopefully the evidence would help JC press the right buttons to break open one of the Kaufmans or else give him leads to follow in a different direction.

Until then, he was on his own.

He'd keep grinding away. The Kaufman kids, neighbors, work associates, anyone he could find with a connection—he'd work on all of them.

He considered the final Kaufman sibling as he threaded through the streets beyond Sun Country golf course. Jeremy lived in a mobile home park near the railroad. Did the guy need money or was the place just convenient to his job with the railroad? Either way, Jeremy lived and worked within a few miles of the casino, the crime scene, the airport where his brother-in-law was employed, and the car dealership where his brother worked.

Sometimes coincidence—and life—was a real bitch.

JC parked beside a late model Toyota pickup and checked in with Dispatch. He peered through the rig's window—neat and empty inside—and then studied the mobile homes while he talked. Several of the sites had neat lawns and trees, the trailers decked out with awnings and porches. There'd been no effort to make Jeremy's place look like anything other than what it was—an impersonal, inexpensive place to live. No underpinning around the trailer's base. No grass, flowers or any other kind of decoration.

A tall, lean man answered the door on the first knock.

"You the cop?"

JC nodded and introduced himself.

"Come on in." Jeremy turned, picked up a remote and killed the television.

Following him, JC watched as the guy closed the battered entertainment cabinet, concealing a high-end system.

"Have a seat." Jeremy sat on the sofa, leaving JC

the choice of joining him on the sofa or sitting in the leather recliner with his back to the door. A faint grin curved his mouth as if he knew it would kill JC to sit in a vulnerable position where someone could walk up behind him.

JC chose the sofa.

Like his brothers and sister, Jeremy was a blue-eyed blond, but his features were narrower and harder. He was taller than his brothers, closer to JC's six-foot height.

He also gave off the same faintly guilty vibe as his siblings.

"Want a beer?"

"No thanks."

"Mind if I finish mine?"

Alcohol could tarnish anything the guy said. "How about put it in the 'fridge and finish it later."

Jeremy poured the last inch of beer into the sink and reclaimed his seat.

They covered the ground JC had hit with the guy's siblings. No conflicts. No enemies.

"My dad was a good man." Jeremy leaned forward, bracing his forearms on his thighs. "Whatever it takes. Wherever it goes, find out who did this."

"Where do you think it might go?"

Jeremy shook his head.

"Tell me about your family." JC changed tactics.

"Family." He sighed, rubbed his hands together. "Mom was the one who held things together. No...that sounds wrong." He straightened. "You grow up around here?"

JC nodded.

"Then you know what it's like. Dad was at the

Labs. Mom was at home. It was the fuckin' American Dream. She volunteered everywhere. Had snacks ready when we got home from school and dinner on the table when Dad walked through the door." He raked fingers through his hair. "Don't get me wrong. We had a great childhood. My parents were the best. Ryan and I were close. We're only a year apart. We did the hunting/fishing/football thing. Jess was Mom's... clone? The girl she wanted. Owen...Jeeze, he's the classic youngest kid. Anyway, when Ryan and I were in college, pretty much out of the house, Dad went from casual gambling to making it a serious pursuit. He was good. Really good. He went out on the tour and made a ton of money. But he didn't really care about it. Know what I mean?"

"Tell me."

"Nothing changed when he started winning. They lived in the same house. Did the same stuff they'd always done. It wasn't about the money."

"The challenge?"

Jeremy nodded. "Not long after he started winning big, Mom got sick. Cancer. Dad came home to be with her. Sure, the money helped pay for doctors and crap, but it didn't keep Mom from dying." He stopped and looked away.

JC waited. He kept his posture loose and open. *Keep talking.*

"Dad was sorta lost after that. Yeah, Ryan and Jess have him over for dinner. I take him fishing. But...he was lonely. You know what's happening at the Labs. Everything's a contract. People are scrambling. Moving from here to South Carolina to White Sands to wherever they can pick up the next project. His old friends aren't around. The people he and Mom did stuff with moved on after she died. If that chick at the casino made him happy, who cares? It was his money. If he wanted to give it to her, it was his choice."

"Did he tell you he was giving her money?"

Jeremy shook his head. "Nope. But Ryan, Jess and Owen are convinced she's going to screw them over."

JC glanced around the living area. Most of the furnishings were crap but in addition to the hidden television, tiny Bose speakers sat on top of the cabinet and the recliner was a leather ergonomic number that made his back twinge with a covetous desire. He suspected Jeremy paid for the things that were important to him and could give a damn about the rest of it. He also had the feeling the guy was holding back, waiting for him to ask the right question, push the right button. He forced his hands to stay open and relaxed while he desperately tried to figure out what the trigger might be. "You don't care about the money?"

One shoulder twitched. "I make a good living. Working nights means I can head out during the day, hunt whatever's in season. I got what I need."

"What kind of guns do you have?"

A sardonic smile tilted Jeremy's mouth. "A Benelli 12 and a Winchester 30-30."

A nice shotgun and an older lever-action rifle. "No handguns?"

"Nope. Never saw the need."

Easy enough to check. Washington state was good about gun registrations. "You said you have what you need. Does that include a woman?"

"Not right now. Nobody special anyway. If I

find the right person, I have money saved to give her more than this."

JC studied him. Jeremy was either the most level headed of the Kaufman kids or a sociopath. At a gut level, he kinda liked the guy so he hoped Jeremy wasn't blowing smoke up his ass.

"When are you going to ask me where I was Thursday night?" One eyebrow rose above that crooked grin.

"Where were you Friday morning, between one and five?"

"At work."

"Can anyone verify that?"

Jeremy clasped his hands, ground the palms together. "Probably. Most of it, anyway. We had a problem with the hydraulics, middle of the shift, which would make it around two. I'd have to check my paperwork for the exact time. Took a couple of hours to clear. It was quiet after that. I stayed in the office reading."

"Alone?"

"Couple guys came in to help with the hydraulics job. They hung around for a while. Some people walked through the office to get coffee. Couldn't tell you who it was." He shrugged and leaned back. "Just a typical night."

"So you could've left and no one would notice."

"I probably could've. But I didn't."

"So basically you have no alibi for at least part of the night."

"Guess not. For the record, though, I did not kill my father."

# CHAPTER TEN

Maddie loved Mondays. It was always a day off work and a day she could spend with Caden. Generally she did her homework while he was at pre-school. She'd also discovered the library had story time which fit neatly into their schedule and gave her a chance to use the library computer.

She peered around the cubicle's dividing panel and made sure Caden was happily engaged in the reading circle before opening an Internet window. After a restless night of tossing and turning, today the thing with Owen bugged her as much as it scared her. The idea that the police could just keep you in jail *really* bugged her. She typed, "How long can the police hold you after they arrest you?" into the search window.

Pages of links filled the screen. She clicked the first one.

*The right to a speedy trial is guaranteed to criminal defendants by the Sixth Amendment to the U.S. Constitution. A "speedy trial" means the defendant must be tried for the alleged crimes within a reasonable time after being arrested.*

Okay. Constitutional right sounded good. So what was reasonable and what was a speedy trial?

*The state has 48 hours (if there was no warrant for the arrest) or 72 hours (if there was an arrest warrant) from the time of arrest either to bring the person before a magistrate or release them on bond.*

Holy smokes! The police could hold you for two days before they even arrested you?

*Within 48-72 hours, the person will be taken before a judge. The judge will inform him or her of the charges and their rights. At this time, bond may be set (unless the person is charged with a crime that is only bondable in front of a superior court judge).*

Maddie drummed her fingers on the wooden desk. Clearly Owen could be out in a day or so. She didn't know if the judge held court on Sunday but figured for something as simple as a fistfight, they'd release him today.

*After the person is arrested, a prosecutor will review the case before making an independent decision as to what charges should be filed. A prosecutor is not bound by the initial*

*charging decision, but may later*
*change the charged crimes once more*
*evidence is obtained.*

Hmm... The detective had mentioned holding Owen to keep him from causing more trouble. Was the in-jail hold because the police thought Owen killed his father? Was arresting him for throwing a punch at Frank a way to keep him locked up while they wrapped up their murder investigation?

She couldn't do anything about the investigation, but she had a more personal concern. If Owen was bailed out, how was she going to keep him away from her—away from Caden? She glanced over and made sure her son was still caught up in the story.

Would that detective tell her when Owen was released? She jotted a note to call him.

The clock confirmed she had a few minutes before reading time wrapped up. One more area piqued her curiosity. Opening a new search tab, she Googled "estate settlement in Washington State." Daniel's kids and the detective seemed to think Daniel had left something to her in his will.

She didn't believe it. Why would he?

Although it would be nice to add a little money to her tuition saving account.

New links filled the screen. She tapped on a few but didn't understand most of the posted material. It seemed complicated and drawn out. Apparently the attorney—or the personal representative—contacted the beneficiaries to let them know they'd inherit. Settling the estate—actually paying out—looked like it could take a while.

And that was if things went smoothly.

Well, she'd know soon enough if the Kaufman anger was totally misplaced or if Daniel had included her in his will. She closed down the computer, stashed her books in her satchel, and stepped into the children's area.

Other parents were also collecting chattering preschoolers.

"Did you have fun?" Maddie swung Caden onto her hip.

"We read about dinosaurs."

Caden's other obsession.

He drew his fingers into Tyrannosaurus claws and waved them around. "G-roar!"

"Did the big dinosaur remember to thank the nice reading lady?"

Caden twisted around and nearly took a header as he waved his claws at the librarian. "G-roar. Thanks!"

The librarian laughed. "See you next week, little T. Rex."

"Stay beside me." She set Caden down and checked out a handful of books for each of them. He chattered about the stories as they made their way to the parking lot. She peered up and down the rows. Where was her Civic?

Oh, right. She gave a mental head smack. She was driving her mother's car.

Caden trotted beside her toward the Subaru. As they approached it, she noticed a piece of paper fluttering under the windshield wiper.

"Darn it," she muttered. A parking ticket? Her budget had taken enough hits this week. She opened the back door, and settled Caden in his carseat.

Wait a minute. They didn't give parking tickets

in the library lot. It must be one of those annoying ads. She grabbed the paper and tossed the folded flyer on the back seat.

"What's this say?" Caden held up the paper.

She slid behind the wheel, then reached over the seat, took the flyer and smoothed out the crumpled page.

She slid behind the wheel and smoothed out the crumpled paper.

A single line of text centered the page. *You killed him for money. You'll pay for it.*

What the hell? The blood drained from her head. Her vision blurred and her hands shook. She gave an instinctive left, right scan but saw only a few other parents and kids from the reading circle.

"Mommy?"

She swallowed. "It's okay. It's nothing."

Her gaze returned to the threatening note.

Owen was in jail.

Now somebody else was threatening her.

And they knew how to find her.

# CHAPTER ELEVEN

JC met the forensic tech, a woman named Susan Abetya, at the department garage. Short and curvy, she worked twice as hard as the other techs in order to be taken seriously. He'd been pleased to see her name attached to the initial forensic reports.

Kaufman's Lexus had a forlorn, abandoned air about it now that the techs had finished their work. The initial reports had noted fingerprints from all four of the victim's children, their spouses and kids inside the car.

"You didn't find anything from Madeline Larsson?" JC followed Abetya toward the car.

"Nope. And other than the blood smears, the car was only minimally wiped down."

He'd noticed the smears on the driver's seat when he'd inspected the original scene. Could've been the victim moving around as he died. Could be something else. "Tell me about the smears."

"That's why I brought you out here." She stopped beside the open driver's door. "The photos are in my report, but I'm not sure they give you the overall impact."

JC glanced at his copy of the report. He knew how thorough Susan was. There'd be photos from every angle and at every range, from scene-establishing to close up detail.

She beckoned him closer. "Look at the patterns. The blood and tissue splatter is consistent with him being shot in the face while he was sitting behind the wheel. Someone made an attempt"—she pointed at faint smears on the window and door panel—"to clean here."

"But not the rest of the interior."

She shrugged. "Could've been worried about it being seen. Might not've noticed the splatter on the seats. Either way, the body was moved to the passenger seat but placed on something that mostly shielded the seat. "

"You mean like a tarp?" Now that the body was gone, he could see the smears on the driver's seat slid toward the passenger seat. The right side of the car had only a few spots of blood.

"Or something as simple as a plastic trash bag. There's also blood here and here." The tech indicated the seat belt and the crease at the passenger side headrest. "We're testing, but I suspect it's all the victim's."

JC considered the effort required to move a body, especially within the confines of a car. "Okay. Shot at an unknown location. Moved to the passenger seat."

"Which the killer thoughtfully covered."

JC folded his arms. "I always bring trash bags to my midnight meetings."

"Yeah, you're a serious trash-talker," she laughed. "Of course, given this additional smearing, whoever drove the car either sat on another seat cover or else has some 'splaining to do about blood smears on their ass."

"Love to hear that one."

"It'd be a bitch." She pointed at the passenger seat. "Okay. The body was buckled in and taken past the airport to the dumpsite. The seat was upright when the vehicle came in, but I suspect it was reclined for that trip. The blood ran straight back under the head rest."

"Whoever did this had balls of steel. Even at that hour, driving around with a dead man." He grimaced and shook his head.

"You've narrowed it to a male suspect?"

"Nope. But of the people in our suspect pool, I'd say it was more likely a male who moved the body around inside the car."

She nodded. "Makes sense. It's not just the weight, but also the awkward leverage inside the vehicle. Since the victim was found in the driver's seat, at some point he was moved back. That's this second set of smears. Notice the blood was tackier. The consistency's different so the smear pattern's different."

"Deserted location. Middle of the night. Time to do all the repositioning after the fact. But how did the first transfer go unnoticed?" JC rubbed a hand over his jaw. "Where was he when the killer shot him?"

"Can't tell you where that happened, but it definitely wasn't in the parking lot where you found him. The body's final position didn't line up with the blood splatter from the kill shot. Those smears confirm the repositioning." Susan tucked her hands into her pockets. "There's also what *isn't* here. The steering wheel should have Mr. Kaufman's prints."

Should. A statement, not a question. "And the killer's."

She nodded. "Same for the door handles on both sides."

"So we have evidence of movement, but by who?"

Abetya closed the car door. "That's your part."

"I'm on it." JC turned toward the exit, then stopped and faced Susan. "I haven't seen the property list yet. Did you find a blue poker chip in the car?"

She frowned. "No, nothing like that. Why?"

"The victim supposedly had a special chip with him."

Another of those annoying details which could mean nothing at all.

Susan shrugged and headed toward the office tucked into the corner of the garage.

JC crossed the parking lot and entered the department's conference room. For a long time, he studied the whiteboards. The panels detailed the timeline, evidence details, the possible suspects—and all the open questions. He added a few notes about the car, then poked his head into the squad room. "Nunez, got a minute?"

Nunez rose and stretched. "Whatcha need?"

"Someone to bounce ideas off. I got too many suspects and not enough evidence."

"Okay." Nunez studied the board. "Who can you eliminate?"

"The kids were real quick to point at Madeline Larsson."

"But?"

"Solid alibi. With a disabled car and a time-stamped security tape of it, she didn't have time to shoot Kaufman and move the body before witnesses place her in her parents' home." Ironically enough, her car not starting gave her an alibi, as did Phalen with the damn tow truck.

"What was to stop her sneaking out of her parents' house? Taking their car?"

"Logistics. Time. Plus, I doubt she's strong enough to move the body, much less do it without getting blood all over herself."

"Could she have cleaned up after herself? Laundry and a shower would take care of a lot of evidence." Nunez tugged at his lower lip. "Still be trace if you had enough to get a warrant."

"Her mother confirmed Madeline was wearing the clothes she'd worn to work at the casino when she woke her Friday morning."

"You don't sound convinced she's clear."

JC shrugged. "The victim's kids have pushed so hard, I want to make sure I'm not leaving an opening for a defense attorney to wiggle through."

"If not her, who? The kids?"

JC folded his arms and leaned against the wall beside the white board. "If the motive isn't sex, money is usually second on the list. The victim had enough money to tempt a lot of people and his children are already counting it."

"Family love," Nunez snorted.

"Yeah. I talked with the victim's attorney. He confirmed they're beneficiaries."

"Think the will might shake something loose?"

"The attorney's notifying them today. Usually he'd just mail the standard forms. You know, an 'I'm the personal representative; you're a beneficiary' thing. The kicker is they have the right to contest the will."

"Think that's going to be an issue?"

JC nodded. "Money seems to be the stick up their ass. They think their dad cut them out and left everything to the girl."

"Guy had money?"

"Lots of it."

Nunez gave a low whistle. "No wonder you're triple-checking her alibi."

A grin twisted JC's mouth. "Wouldn't you love to be at that meeting with the lawyer?"

"No shit. You have anything implicating one of the kids?"

"Not yet, but at this point, my focus is on the family." He recapped his interviews with the victim's children.

Nunez propped a hip against a desk. "Not a robbery?"

"Nope. Nothing missing except his poker chip."

"Why would they take that?"

"Good question." He explained about the tour chip.

"So at this point, it could've been any one of them."

"Or two of them working together. Owen was mad about the money tap cutting off. We already know he was angry enough to hit the old man."

"Was he pissed enough to kill him?"

"A neighbor heard the yelling and saw Owen tear off in his truck, but didn't see him hit his dad. Dumbass went after Madeline at the casino and hit one of the security guys."

"Dumbass is right."

"We asked for a 72-hour hold. For a simple assault, he'd already be out. With the homicide question hanging and Owen a suspect, there's a lot of moving pieces to consider."

"What'd the PA say?"

"He isn't sure if—or what—they're going to file. They may sit on the assault charge and see what happens with our investigation. Best I can hope for is the judge sets bail instead of personal recognizance. Might slow him down a little." JC shook his head. "Guy's a loose cannon. If the victim did leave money to the girl, he could go after her again. We're running a protective order past the judge today. Maybe that'll help on the bail decision too."

"What about the others?"

"Ryan, Christopher and Jeremy all work within a five mile radius of each other, the casino, and the building where the victim was found. Christopher and Jeremy especially would be familiar with that area of town. None of them have alibis for at least part of the window the ME gave us."

"Could be any of them."

"Or to keep it interesting, any one of them could've shot the dad and then gone to the others for help covering it up."

"Good thing this is your clusterfuck and not mine." Nunez pushed away from the desk.

"There's one more thing."

Nunez paused. "Yeah?"

"I attended the autopsy this morning before I met Abetya." Damn, everything about autopsies sucked. The smell, the carving up of what used to be a person. The indignity of it all.

"And?" Nunez prodded when he didn't

continue.

"The victim had cancer. Advanced cancer. I checked with his personal physician. He hadn't told his kids."

Nunez's lips twisted as he seemed to consider the possibilities. "Think he set himself up to do suicide by someone else? He could've wanted a quick end."

"Possible. It's still murder."

Nunez broadened his stance. A thoughtful expression thinned his lips and drifted his gaze. "Why wouldn't he tell them? Most people want that...support...help...sympathy..."

JC shrugged. "If I had to guess, he didn't tell them because his wife died of cancer a couple of years ago. Apparently it was brutal there at the end. The victim's doctor said Kaufman turned down chemo. Said he didn't want to drag it out and be miserable just to maybe get a couple more months."

"Probably didn't want anyone doing a death watch over him."

"Maybe." JC sighed. "I've seen that attitude in older people"—he'd seen it with his grandfather—"especially if the spouse is already gone. They're done. Ready to go. But this guy was pretty young."

Nunez scratched his jaw. "It could explain why the girl, Madeline, is a beneficiary. If the vic knew he was dying, it's easier to put it in the will instead of dealing with the arguments over a flat-out gift. Any idea how much she's getting?"

"Nope. The attorney only said she's a beneficiary."

"So we're back to Owen doing something stupid."

CATHY PERKINS

"Or one of the others doing something just as dumb." JC blew out a long sigh. "I gotta nail down or blow up these guys' alibis."

# CHAPTER TWELVE

*Monday afternoon*

"It's creepy." Maddie trapped her phone between her shoulder and ear. She tossed Legos in a tub and glanced at Caden. He was wrapped up in a PBS rerun of *Reading Rainbow*. She lowered her voice. "Someone left a threatening note on my windshield. The windshield of my mother's car. Who even knows I'm driving it?"

"Your life is like some crazy reality TV show," Lauren's voice had that horrified can't-look-away-from-the-train-wreck tone. "What did it say?"

She tossed more Legos into the bucket and collected the empty snack dishes. She and Caden had built a town after lunch. Then T. Rex stomped through and destroyed all the buildings. Caden had promptly used his firetruck to save everybody. Part of her regretted mentioning the note to Lauren, but it did have her a little weirded out. "Stuff about Daniel. About the money."

"Did you tell the cops?"

"Well, duh? Of course."

"And?"

"There's nothing they can do except take the note and stick it in the file." Balancing the empty popcorn bowl and juice glasses, she rounded the peninsula into the kitchen and placed the dishes in the sink.

"Be careful," Lauren said. "That guy at the Tom Tom was bat-shit crazy. You think he's doing it?"

"He's in jail." At least she thought Owen was still in jail. She turned on the faucet and rinsed the dishes. Over the sound of running water, she heard hammering on the front door.

"Open the door, Maddie."

"Damn." She grabbed a towel. "It's Asher. I better go."

"If he gives you any crap, call the cops," Lauren warned.

"I know you're in there." The words were loud, angry and slurred.

"Dammit." She dried her hands and tossed the towel on the counter. From the sound of it, Asher had been drinking.

"I saw the newspaper. You're a murder suspect. I should haul your ass back to court. You aren't a fit mother."

"You're so full of bull," she muttered under her breath. She didn't kill anybody. No way was he getting Caden away from her.

Another series of blows landed on the front door. "Open the goddamn door."

She'd caved to Asher's threats and demands too many times in the past. She'd tried to let him be part of Caden's life, thinking her son needed to know his father. Now she realized exposing Caden to Asher wasn't helpful. The bruise on Daniel's face had made her face reality—a reality she'd ignored when she was the target. Someone being 'family' didn't guarantee

104

they weren't toxic. Asher wasn't a father figure she wanted her son using as a role model.

Caden ran across the living room, wide-eyed. "Daddy's here."

"Let's stay in the kitchen. Daddy isn't in a good mood today."

He turned and made a beeline for the front door. "Daddy."

"Caden, come here." Still clutching her phone, she raced into the hall after him.

Caden raised both hands and tugged at the doorknob. Thank goodness she'd locked it after the police officer left with the windshield note.

"He wants to see me." Asher pounded on the door. "Dammit, open the damn door."

She snatched up her son. "The party was yesterday. Go home, Asher."

"Open the door, bitch." The voice vicious, the blows were lower now, as if he was kicking the door.

Caden struggled against her restraint. "Mommy. Let me down."

"If you don't leave right now, I'm calling the police. You know you're violating our agreement on your drinking." Her hands trembled and she nearly lost her hold on her child.

"Daddy."

The plaintive tone broke her heart. Why did Asher have to be such an ass?

Asher had used Caden too many times to get to her, to force her to give him money, food, a place to stay. No more. Struggling to hang onto the squirming boy, her fingers flew across the phone screen. Taking a deep breath, refusing to think about how Asher was going to react, she pressed 911.

"911. What is your emergency?"

"My ex-husband is pounding on the front door, kicking it. I'm scared for both my son and myself." She let the quaver in her voice show. Being honest about her fear might bring the cops faster.

A crash came from the rear of the house. She shrieked, whirled and stepped forward, peering toward the noise. Glass littered the kitchen floor.

Caden clutched her shirt and wailed.

Asher's hand reached through the broken window and unlocked the door. "I told you to let me in," he yelled.

"Ma'am, are you in danger?"

"Yes!" She raced to her bedroom, slammed and locked the door. "He's in the house."

"Where are you and where is he?"

"I've got my child. We're in the bedroom. I don't know exactly where Asher is. Maybe the kitchen. He broke that door."

"A patrol officer is enroute. Please stay on the phone with me."

She clutched the phone as if it were a lifeline. "Please hurry."

She heard slamming noise from the front of the house. Please don't tear up the house again. She cuddled Caden. "It'll be okay."

"Why's Daddy mad?" he sobbed.

"I don't know, Sweetie. It's not your fault."

Footsteps sounded and the bedroom door rattled. "Quit playing games. Where'd you hide your tip money?"

"The cops are coming."

"You wouldn't do that." His laugh was harsh and mocking.

She hadn't followed through in the past. Once they'd divorced, he'd held up his end of the agreement and gone to AA. Until last week.

And apparently this week.

A siren sounded in the distance, the sound rapidly growing louder.

"Hurry," she breathed.

"I want to see Caden."

Her son, who'd been so eager to see his daddy moments earlier, clung to her. "Go away, Asher. We're all tired. You aren't supposed to be here when you've been drinking. You're scaring Caden."

The siren stopped and moments later, a different voice called from the rear of the house. "Police."

The bedroom door shuddered as Asher kicked it. "You bitch. I'll get you for this."

"Step away from the door. Hands behind your head," an authoritarian voice demanded.

"This is my house. It's my kid's birthday. I have a right to be here."

Asher's belligerent tone was overridden by the officer. "On the floor. Now."

Scuffling noises came through the door. Maddie rocked Caden, crooning soothing sounds, hoping her own distress wasn't leaking through and making things worse.

"She can't keep me away from my kid."

Actually, she could.

And she would.

She wasn't living with Asher's threats any longer.

# CHAPTER THIRTEEN

JC cruised through Daniel Kaufman's neighborhood. He'd interviewed the victim's friends, former co-workers, neighbors and poker tour players. Other than the comments about Owen, he hadn't learned much that could help his investigation. There were a couple of neighbors he still needed to catch.

He slowed in front of Kaufman's gray-sided house. An older section of Pasco, the neighborhood was filled with neat bungalows and small, one-story ranchers. Mature trees grew in the strip between the street and the sidewalk. Unusual in the Tri-Cities' windy, dry climate, the trees still held a few colorful leaves.

Nice area.

A few places had only bare grass inside a chain link fence, but most of the homes had small trees and shrubs planted in the yard. In general, the yards had been recently mowed. Some of the houses—Kaufman's included—had shrubs and trees that needed trimming. A frown twitched JC's lips. Overgrown shrubbery was a burglar's favorite hiding place and older people were too easy a target. Where were these old people's kids?

While several houses had a car or two parked on

the street out front, most residents parked in garages reached by a narrow alley behind the houses. JC nosed the unmarked into the alley behind Kaufman's place, checking the pullouts and driveways as he cruised through. An older Buick four-door stood in the short driveway to the left of Kaufman's place. The house and car belonged to one of the neighbors who'd been absent over the weekend. JC swung around to the front, parked at the curb, and headed to the door.

A white-haired man, late-sixties, five-nine, maybe a hundred sixty pounds, answered the door.

JC introduced himself.

"Come on in, Detective. I'm Sean Moffat. I bet you're here about Dan Kaufman." He led the way to a neat living room. "Have a seat."

Once they were settled and he'd declined offers of coffee, pop, and water, JC asked, "Did you know Mr. Kaufman?"

"Oh yeah. Our kids grew up together. Hell of a thing. Getting killed sitting in your own car. Can't trust anybody any longer. Why I can remember when we didn't bother to lock our doors."

"Mr. Moffat." JC steered the guy back to the investigation. "Did you notice anything unusual about Mr. Kaufman? See anyone or anything different at or around his house?"

"Things were usually pretty calm over there, but man, he had a rip-roaring argument with his son." Moffat gave a disapproving headshake.

"With Owen?"

"Nah." Moffat dismissed his question with a flap of his hand. "That was earlier in the week. Besides, you said 'anything unusual.' Dan and Owen argued all the time. He's been staying over there, you know."

"Who is?"

"Owen."

JC filed the detail away. As far as he could tell, Owen had no permanent address. Free rent—and food—would've been irresistible to him. "Tell me about this 'unusual argument.'"

"Let's see. It was Wednesday evening." Moffat leaned back, settling into a storytelling pose. "I was just getting home that day. I worked a little late and then had to get groceries. Social Security doesn't stretch as far as it used to. I'm working part-time at the office supply store. Anyway, I had several bags of groceries, even if it's just me living here now. I'm a pretty good cook." He patted his belly.

"The Kaufmans?" JC prodded. The old man gave off a lonely vibe. While he sympathized, he saw the man as the kind who would talk all afternoon—without saying anything—if it kept an audience around. He didn't want to be rude, but he needed to keep the guy focused. His instincts were telling him, this *unusual* argument could be important.

"Oh, yeah. The oldest boy. Ryan. I noticed his car was parked out front when I got home. I didn't think anything about it at first. Dan usually goes to church with them—Ryan and his family—on Wednesdays. Anyway, like I said, Ryan was here when I arrived. I pulled around back like I always do. Man, I could hear the raised voices the minute I stepped out of the car. They must've been in the family room with the slider open. A lot of people are replacing those old sliders with those French doors, but the sliders are a lot more secure." He lifted a hand, as if holding off an argument. "I know you can

110

lift out the cheap sliders but these houses were built solid."

"Any idea what they were arguing about?" JC nudged him back on topic.

"Nope. Less than a minute later, while I was still unpacking my groceries, Ryan went storming out and drove off." He gestured to the framed opening between the living room and an eat-in kitchen. "You can see straight through from the kitchen in these houses. Used to be real helpful when we had a yard full of kids to keep track of."

"Did you talk to Mr. Kaufman after his argument with Ryan?"

"Nah. It was a family thing. I didn't want to interfere." He stopped. A thoughtful expression slid across his wrinkled face. "Kinda wish I had now. I guess it was only a couple days later that Dan was killed."

JC asked more questions, but got nothing new. He spent a few minutes letting the guy reminisce about the kids growing up in the neighborhood and how much it had all changed. After wrapping up the interview, he walked next door to the Kaufman residence. Either Owen wasn't there or was lying low.

Keeping an eye on the place, he returned to his car and pulled out his laptop. Holly had teased him during his last homicide investigation—one of the nine million times she'd tried to change the subject when she was sticking her nose in where it didn't belong—by calling the unmarked vehicle his mobile office. He glanced at the laptop and mobile printer. She had a point.

He toyed with his phone, wondering if he could

call her at work or if she was as busy as he was. Cancelling their plans this past weekend meant he hadn't seen her in nearly a week.

With a sigh, he set the phone aside and booted the computer. Missing Holly was another reason he really needed to wrap up this investigation and get his own life back.

Maddie curled up on the sofa and stared at the textbook that mocked her from the ottoman. *Finish your homework.*

She knew she should be studying, but *tired* didn't begin to describe how exhausted she felt. Calming Caden after the ugly episode with Asher had taken forever. Even the neighbor who helped her nail a piece of plywood over the broken back door window hadn't distracted him. He'd finally crashed on the sofa.

A nap sounded so appealing.

Her cell's ring tone broke the silence. Heartrate skyrocketing, she grabbed the phone before the noise woke her son. She stared at the unfamiliar number displayed on the phone screen. She'd been holding her breath for hours, half-expecting Asher to call, demanding she bail him out of jail. He'd ranted at her the entire time the cop was slapping cuffs on him and hauling him away.

"Hello?" She cringed at the tentative tone that emerged. She wanted—*needed*—to stay assertive.

"Is this Madeline Larsson?"

"Who's calling?" She straightened.

"My name is Nick Favero. I'm an attorney here

in town."

Seriously? She lowered her hand and stared at the phone. Asher had already hired an attorney to come after her? He'd moved that fast?

Fine.

"Asher was in violation of our agreement. We have nothing to discuss."

"I'm not sure who Asher is, but I'm calling on behalf of Daniel Kaufman's estate."

"Oh." Her checks warmed. Way to sound like an idiot. Wait. Daniel's estate?

"I'm the personal representative for the estate. Normally, I would send you a letter, informing you about the initial steps in the process, but under the unusual set of circumstances, I've been asked to accelerate and expedite the initial notification."

She was learning to parse sentences. "Who asked you to do this?" Were his kids that eager to find out what they would inherit? It sounded rather crass to her.

"The authorities—law enforcement—suggested it. I've arranged a meeting tomorrow afternoon for all the beneficiaries. Is that time convenient for you?"

"I'm a beneficiary?" *Daniel left something to me?*

The attorney gave a small chuckle. "That is the point of this call. Notifying the beneficiaries."

"Wow. Didn't see that coming." She raked her fingers through her hair. In spite of his kids' nasty comments, she hadn't expected a gift. "What time is your meeting? I have a class at two and then I have to be at work at five."

"I've set it for 1 PM to accommodate lunch schedules and those of you who work late shifts."

She took a deep breath. "I'll be there. Thank you for calling."

Whoa. She slowly lowered the phone. Daniel left her something in his will?

Why would he do that?

Sure, it would be nice if he left her some money. Who didn't secretly wish they had a childless rich uncle? But Daniel had a family. How would they feel about a gift to her?

She groaned. She knew how they felt. They were pissed as all get out.

Of course it was Daniel's money to do with as he pleased. With his murder, however, and as crazy as this week had been, she couldn't help but worry. Was the baggage attached to Daniel's generosity going to complicate her life in ways she couldn't fully imagine?

JC dodged the multiple sales people who wanted to sell him a car. He gave each a brisk smile and nod and kept walking purposefully toward Ryan Kaufman's office. He wanted answers to two primary questions. What had Ryan argued with his father about and why had he lied about it?

Those answers could open a host of new questions.

He found the man talking with another employee in the hallway of the office corridor.

Ryan stepped away from the other guy. "Detective? Has there been a break in the case?"

"Could we talk in your office? I need to clear up a few details."

"Sure." Ryan glanced at his co-worker. "I'll catch

you later, Manan."

JC followed Ryan past the small conference rooms, which were used to negotiate car sales, into a small office. A laminate-topped peninsula separated the office into two parts. A desk and wall mount cabinets defined the rear work area. A couple of uncomfortable-looking chairs stood on the door side of the space. Generic pictures of shiny cars and the Columbia River studded the walls.

"What can I do for you?" Ryan dropped into a faux leather manager chair. He stacked some papers, clearing the space between them.

JC crossed an ankle over his knee and adopted a casual pose. The craptastic chair meant it took more effort than usual. "I need your help sorting out a few things. Mostly, I'm confused about the timeline. Trying to place who was where. You said your Dad went to church with you on Wednesday, but other people tell me he wasn't there."

"You're right." A chagrinned smile twitched Ryan's mouth. "I didn't think that through. It was such a shock, hearing about Dad. I just gave you the usual routine. Then when I thought about it later, I realized Dad didn't go that week and why he didn't go..."

He waited.

"I should've called you." Ryan sighed. "I didn't want you to get the wrong idea about my dad, like he was a scuzzy, criminal gambler. He was a good man. A great father. I should've told you he didn't want to go to church with us that Wednesday. Clearly you've already figured that out."

"Why not? I thought"—he caught himself before he said *the victim*—"your father enjoyed doing stuff with you and your family."

"He did." Ryan pulled a hand across his face. "God. What a mess. Dad didn't want to go because..." He shifted and straightened the stack of papers. "Owen showed up at my house at dinnertime on Wednesday, looking for money." He pushed the paperwork aside and he shook his head. "I told him to go get a job and earn his own."

"Reasonable," JC agreed.

"And I told him we weren't hiring. The last thing I need around here is a deadbeat brother." Ryan's gaze drifted, slowly skating over the office's furnishings before coming to rest on the desk. "Kid's always had it too easy. Mom and Dad treated him like a baby and he's still acting like one. Anyway, when I wouldn't give him money, Owen started ranting about Dad cutting him off."

Ryan lifted his gaze and met JC's eyes. "I didn't want to hear it. Know what I mean? Kid needs to grow up and act like an adult. When I finally got rid of him, I realized it was time to leave for church and Dad hadn't shown up. I called. No answer, so I went over there." He shrugged. "Partly to make sure he was okay and partly to find out what the hel—what was going on. I walked in and found my father sitting in a recliner with a black eye."

He broke eye contact. His fingers stretched to the paperwork and toyed with the corner. "I lost it. I asked if Owen hit him. He wouldn't say. I yelled at Dad for refusing to call the cops. Not exactly how I would've envisioned my last conversation with my father."

Sounded good except the timing was wrong. The argument with Owen had to have been the prior week if the bruise had yellowed on Thursday when Madeline saw Daniel. JC had heard so many lies over the years. All he had to do was watch and listen and he'd pick up on the tell. Ryan's was the papers on his desk. Every time he wandered over into shades of the truth, his fingers meandered to the stack of paperwork.

"Your brother hit your dad?"

Ryan grimaced and pushed the papers away. "Owen asked Dad for money and Dad said no. The kid admitted it. Said he lost his temper. Acted without thinking it through."

JC waited a beat but Ryan left the papers alone. "Think Owen could get mad enough to pull a gun?"

Ryan shrugged. "I don't even know if he owns one."

Interesting that he didn't deny that Owen could shoot their father. Only deflected, making the question about gun ownership. "Do you?"

Ryan jerked like someone had tasered him. A scowl darkened his face. "Are you asking if I shot my father?"

"I asked if you owned a gun."

"I've owned a hunting rifle since I was a kid. Not that I have time to hunt anymore. The rifle's locked up at the house because I have two kids and I don't have time to teach them—" He abruptly closed his mouth and glared at JC.

"So if Owen was looking for a weapon, he wouldn't have come to you." JC made it a statement.

Ryan did what JC expected. He took a deep breath, straightened the papers, and said. "No. Owen didn't ask me for a pistol."

"So you argued with your father about Owen?

117

The assault?"

He nodded. "I wish I'd known the whole story that night."

"Oh?"

"I don't know if it would've made a difference or not." Ryan poked at the papers. Grimaced. "It's a bitch trying to focus on work when all I can think about is Dad."

"That's understandable. There are stages to grief and the loss of a parent is a huge shock."

"I wish I'd handled things differently. Done more about Owen or for Dad." He scrubbed his hands over his face. "You might as well hear the rest of our sordid family secrets." His hands dropped and he looked JC in the eye. "Owen came to me on Friday, yelling about Dad cutting us out of his will. Claiming we didn't deserve his money. That we'd had it easy instead of having to work two jobs like that girl. Well, nobody gave me anything. I've worked my butt off to get where I am." He slammed away from his desk and paced the narrow confine of the office.

Throwing his brother under the bus? "A lot of pressure in your position."

"You don't know the half of it. Every goddamn day it's something." Ryan stopped and took a deep breath. "Forget it. We all have bad days at the office."

He wondered just how much pressure Ryan was under. Or if it was really grief working its way through his system and not a form of guilt.

Ryan reclaimed his seat. "I heard you were there yesterday, at the casino, when Owen got arrested."

"How'd you know about that?" Interesting diversion.

"The loser called me this morning and expected

me to come bail him out of jail."

JC considered this. He wasn't listed as the arresting officer—he'd let one of the patrol officers take over—but he would've been notified if Owen went before the magistrate. The prosecutor had agreed to hold off charging for a day to give them time on the investigation. "Bail probably hasn't been set."

"Good. He belongs in jail."

For what? Being a general asshole? Assaulting Madeline and the Tom Tom's security staff? Hitting his dad?

Or killing him?

JC left the dealership's office area, debating whether he should've pushed harder. At this stage of the investigation, he wanted to be careful. With new information, he could come back at the guy— without him already having his guard up. But damn, how honest had Ryan been? The guy had been carefully constructing a trap for his brother and glossing over his own argument with his dad.

What had he and his father actually argued about on Wednesday? Ryan had teetered on the edge of truth too many times. Owen was undoubtedly part of the argument. Was there more to the conflict? Was Ryan's evasion due to Owen's involvement in the assault? A larger crime?

What did Ryan know—or suspect?

JC stopped at the edge of the sales floor and pretended to examine a shiny new sedan. Did Ryan believe what he'd implied? That Owen could kill their father?

What if Ryan learned about a possible change to his father's will on Wednesday rather than Friday? Owen had ranted about it on Sunday at the casino and according to all his siblings, had made that claim more than once. Had Ryan confronted his father on Wednesday about *that* change rather than arguing over a week-old black eye? The lie about church service attendance could be explained away and, by itself, was inconsequential.

Except it said Ryan lied if he thought it helped his position.

Was it unbelievable that Ryan would cover for his dad's black eye? For his brother's volcanic temper?

JC thought back to the original interview. Ryan had claimed he was at work until midnight on Thursday and then at home with Emily afterwards. JC scanned the sales floor. *Pick a starting point. Find someone to confirm the guy's Thursday night alibi.*

He zeroed in on the woman sitting at the service desk. *Perfect.*

Sliding an easy smile on his face, he sauntered over. She straightened and smiled at him. "Hello. Can I help you?"

He leaned a hip against the counter and crossed his arms. The position bulked out his arms and chest and offered a glimpse of his weapon when his jacket opened. Civilians—especially women—always seemed to be fascinated by it. "How'd your event go this weekend?"

"The Fall Celebration? It went great. Lots of foot-traffic and a sales record. The Big Boss is really happy with everybody."

*Wonder how much pressure Ryan's feeling at work?* "Cars selling well with the economy picking up?"

She nodded. "When gas prices skyrocketed and it looked like Hanford might lose funding, we were really worried." She shuddered. "But things are looking up now."

"Ryan said you were all here late, setting up for your event."

"You mean on Thursday? Yeah, we had the decorations and the kid games and everything to put together. It looked really nice." Her gaze drifted to the showroom floor as if she were still seeing the full event. "Too bad we had to take the games back so fast. We got to keep the decorations."

"That's a lot to set up." He scanned the sales floor as if he were admiring the pumpkins and leaves and junk instead of cataloging the people present. Turning back to her, he added a touch of admiration to his tone. "How long did it take you to do all this?"

"Gosh." She tilted her head and ran a preening hand through her hair. "There were a bunch of us here, so it was kinda fun. Ryan brought in pizza. Don't worry." She gave him a dazzling smile. "We had pop instead of beer. Can't have any impaired drivers."

"We hate that." He returned her grin even as he remembered Ryan had said he went home for dinner with his family. "You must have been here half the night to get all this set up."

"Most people left around ten. When I left at eleven, there were only a few people finishing the details."

JC hooked a thumb toward the office corridor. "Yeah, Ryan said he was here 'til midnight."

She nodded. "Ryan, David, Manan, Travis and Hector were still here when I left."

Manan. He was the guy Ryan was talking to when JC arrived. He jotted down the men's names. "Ryan's dad was killed later that night."

"That's right." Her bright smile faded. "I never met him, but losing a parent. Especially that way..."

"Yeah. It's tough. Look, do you have phone numbers for these guys?" He waved his pen over the names he'd just listed.

"Sure." She tapped around on the computer for a minute, then stopped. Her mouth formed a perfect O as the dots finally connected. She stared at him. "Do you think Ryan had something...that he...?"

JC leaned on the counter, keeping his posture loose and relaxed. "Nah. His wife was asleep when he got home, so I need people who can clear him. Give him an alibi so I can cross him off the list and go after the person who did it."

"Oh. That makes sense." She flashed another brilliant smile and tapped around some more on the computer. Minutes later, he had addresses and phone numbers for all the men she remembered as being at the dealership late Thursday night.

He pulled a business card from his pocket. "If you think of anything else, call me."

"Does it have to be about the case?" She twirled a strand of hair around her finger and looked up at him from under her lashes.

He laughed—keeping it a nice chuckle—and strolled away. There was a reason the only number on the card was for the phone at the station.

# CHAPTER FOURTEEN

*Tuesday morning*

"Got it!" A uniformed officer greeted JC when he walked into the sheriff's department at 07:00.

JC had requested surveillance recordings from businesses located on streets between the dumpsite and town. A couple of deputies, eager for overtime on top of their regular twelve-hour shifts, had fast-forwarded through dozens of tapes. Fortunately there wasn't a huge amount of traffic in the area between midnight and 05:00, although traffic picked up after four. At 04:21, a security camera on 20th Avenue caught the Dodge Ram—and a perfect shot of the guy driving it.

"Good job." JC fist-bumped the kid. "Hensley's probably headed to the airport, but it isn't the route he'd take from his house."

"I'll back up and see if I can find him again."

"If he drove 395, we won't see him, but we might get lucky at one of the onramps. Backtrack him on 20th, though. Maybe we can figure out where he was coming from." JC crossed his arms and considered the possibilities. If Hensley dumped the Lexus and body beyond the airport, what was he doing driving toward the airport from another part of town? Had he stashed the Ram before meeting up with his father-in-law? If so, how did he get back to his truck? And where could he have met the victim? Kaufman's vehicle had vanished shortly after midnight, when he left the Tom Tom casino's parking lot. JC cocked an eyebrow at the deputy. "No luck spotting the victim's Lexus?"

"Not yet."

"Keep trying.

Armed with a downloaded print and his badge, JC headed for the airport. Horizon's morning rush of connecting flights had finished with the 07:00 flight to Portland. The airline didn't have another flight until the 08:49 arrival from Seattle. It took longer to find someone at the ticket counter than it did for the clerk to locate the supervisor. JC flashed his badge and asked to speak to Christopher Hensley.

The door opened a few minutes later and a guy in coveralls stepped out of the controlled area. The supervisor pointed at JC and then vanished through the same door Chris had used.

"Why are you here?" Surprise raised Chris's eyebrows.

JC held up the security photo. "Care to explain this?"

"Shit." Chris raked his fingers through his hair. "It's not what you think."

"What am I thinking?" JC hardened his jaw and his tone.

"Come on." Chris led the way into the empty baggage claim area. Chairs lined the far wall. He dropped into one, his head tilted back against the wall. "I knew this was going to come back to bite me."

"Why?"

"Ryan." The word came out as a groan.

JC waited.

"He called me that night."

"About?" JC asked when Chris didn't continue.

"Where to start." Chris shifted around and finally leaned forward, resting his forearms on his thighs. His fingers dangled and he shook his head.

"Ryan called you."

"Yeah." He took a deep breath. "He called about four and asked me to pick him up near Sun Willows.

"He was at the golf course in the middle of the night? Working on his putting?"

"A woman." Chris sighed. "He said he worked until midnight getting the dealership ready for some promotional thing. I don't know where he met this woman or how long he's been seeing her. I got the impression she was a customer. Anyway, he'd arranged to meet her that night after work. They went out to the golf course in her car. At least he was smart enough to get away from the dealership."

He added under his breath. "The dumbass."

"They do make hotels for those kinds of hookups."

"Yeah." Chris straightened. "I figured out she was married pretty quick too. Otherwise, why pick some empty parking lot like a high school kid? Anyway, they went out on the backside of the golf course and did whatever. Afterward, they're sitting in her car and Ryan tells her it's over, that he feels guilty and all that shit. The idiot can't wait until she drives him back to the dealership and his car."

"Poor planning," JC agreed.

"She kicks him out and drives off. At least he had his clothes on."

"Helpful."

"He started walking and realized there was no way he was going to get back to his car in time to get home before Emily woke up. He knew I'd be up, so he called and asked me to come get him."

JC thought about Ryan's original version of events. Emily had slept until Ryan woke her up, barely in time to get the kids to school. Was she that sound a sleeper? Was a 04:30 arrival less noticeable than one at midnight? "Why didn't you tell me this earlier?"

Chris grimaced. "'Cause my brother-in-law is an idiot?"

"Besides that."

"It wasn't connected to Daniel's murder. Having it come out now is doing exactly what I worried about." A scowl tightened Chris' features. "It makes us look bad, well...worse. Ryan for being an ass, cheating on his wife, and me for helping cover it up. If he was my brother I'd have decked him. I can't even tell Jessica because she thinks her brother walks on water and she does a lot with Emily. I'm gonna feel like an ass every time I see her." Chris shook his head. "I'm so pissed off at the guy."

JC thought about. The story was pretty convenient. A hookup at the golf course? Seriously? There wouldn't be much traffic past Sun Willows at that time of night, but the parking lot was visible from the road. And it was close to where the victim's car and body were found on 4th Avenue out past the airport. "Where exactly did you pick Ryan up?"

"At that coffee shop where Sun Willow Road crosses 20th."

If Ryan was the shooter, then he would've walked down 4th Avenue, skirting the backside of the airport to Stearman. Cutting through the golf course would've kept him off Argent where he'd have been a lot more visible to any traffic.

Or Ryan might simply be a cheating bastard instead of a killer. "What happened after you picked him up?"

"I drove him back to the dealership. Chewed his ass the whole way. Dumped him and headed to work."

"Does this woman have a name?"

"Not that I know."

"Is there anything else you haven't told me?"

"If there's any way not to let Emily and Jessica know about this..." Chris trailed off, eyebrows lifted in a hopeful expression.

"Can't make any promises, but if it isn't relevant." JC shrugged. "They won't hear it from me."

"I gotta get back to work."

"You going to that meeting at the lawyer's office?"

Chris shook his head. "Jess will be there. I think this is just the reading of the will or something like that. If that girl gets everything." He shrugged. "Nothing I can do and Jess's brothers will be there. From what she said, it'll take a while to settle everything, especially if the will's contested. I didn't need to be there today and I'll have to take off work to go to the funeral."

JC would love to be at the meeting with the

attorney, if only to watch the beneficiaries' reactions when the will was read. He rubbed his jaw, considering. If no one posted bail for Owen, maybe he could get the judge to release him into his custody and escort him to the meeting.

But first he had to find a woman.

# CHAPTER FIFTEEN

*Tuesday late-morning*

"Give the money back or you'll regret it." Today's note was as creepy as the earlier one. Maddie scanned the grocery store parking lot. Dozens of cars, a few scattered people, but no one with a flashing sign that read, *"Stalker."*

At least Caden was with the sitter. As always, protecting him was her first instinct. She didn't want any of this ugliness to touch him. She had an hour to finish running errands before the attorney's meeting and her class. Hopefully the meeting would be a short, non-event and she could take Caden to her parents' house before she went to work.

Non-event.

Right.

Facing all the pissed-off Kaufman siblings.

Yeah, that would be a super fun time.

Most likely one of them was leaving the nasty notes, but how could she prove it?

And when was she supposed to fit taking the note to the sheriff's department into today's hectic schedule?

With a sigh she pulled out the detective's card and tapped in the number. The call immediately went to voice mail. "This is Madeline Larsson. I got another one of those notes on my windshield. Uhm...do you want me to hold onto it? Will someone be at the department, uhm, office, later tonight? I can drop it off on my way to work."

She smashed "end." *Gah.* She sounded like an idiot.

With a final shake of her head, she stashed the note in the car and loaded the groceries into the trunk. Another thought struck her as she slammed the truck lid. The landlord hadn't been happy when she reported the broken window. Was she supposed to wait around for the handyman who was coming to repair it? Or would the management company handle it? Nothing had been said about her having to pay for the repair.

She rather wished the landlord would go after Asher for the bill.

Wouldn't that make him even *more* fun to be around?

Maddie parked her mother's car and stared through the windshield at the attorney's white stucco office building. Her hands clenched the steering wheel. What if she put the car in drive and zoomed away. Would it change anything in Daniel's will?

Would it change what these people expected of her?

Her head sagged. Where was she going to find the energy to deal with this meeting?

Her emotions were all tangled up. Daniel's death. All the accusations. Her car. Asher.

Being strong sucked.

Being brave sucked.

Doing what had to be done sucked.

Yeah, yeah.

She was still getting out of the car and going to the meeting.

Minutes later, Maddie checked in with the receptionist who was pleasantly impersonal.

One step at a time.

The woman opened the door to a spacious conference room. "Mr. Favero? Ms Larsson is here."

A middle-aged guy sat at the head of the table. He rose and did the welcome gesture thing so she figured he was the attorney. The rest of the seats were empty.

Please dear God. Tell me there are other beneficiaries. That Daniel left his money mostly to his kids.

She couldn't deal with their anger or her guilt if he hadn't.

She eased around the conference table and perched on the seat to the attorney's left. "The others aren't here yet?"

He shook her hand. "They should be here any minute."

"Thank you," she whispered. Mr. Favero smiled, as if she'd been speaking to him.

A couple appeared at the conference room door. Before the receptionist could announce them, the blond guy who looked a lot like Daniel brushed past her.

"Did you know?" His stunned eyes locked onto the attorney. "Did he tell you?"

"Please sit down, Mr. Kaufman." The attorney

pulled out the chair on his right. "Did I know what?"

The guy pulled in a long breath like he was trying to get his act together. "I talked to the people at the funeral home. They said Dad had cancer. Advanced cancer." He dropped into the chair. His hands shook as he dragged them down his face. "Why didn't he tell us?"

The woman who looked like the moms Maddie saw at Caden's school pulled out a chair and sat beside her husband. "Ryan. I'm sure Daniel had a reason for his decision."

"But it mattered." Ryan's hands slammed onto the table. All of them jumped. "It changes everything."

"Mr. Kaufman," the attorney interjected. "Your father was ill—terminally ill—but his mind was clear. After your mother's illness, he had no desire to prolong either his pain or your heartache. He saw it as sparing you the emotional turmoil of dealing with a lingering death."

Ryan jerked as if someone had goosed him.

"As always," Mr. Favero nodded. "Daniel had your best interest at heart."

Ryan's face crumpled, as if any second he'd burst into tears. Maddie tried to imagine Asher crying over anything or anybody, but couldn't picture it. Maybe the reality of his father's death—or the alternative version after chemo or other gross medical stuff—was finally hitting Ryan.

"I can find my own way."

Maddie cringed when she recognized Owen's voice. She'd expected him to still be in jail. How long head he been out? She straightened and sent a considering gaze at the doorway. Was he the one leaving her threatening notes?

Why hadn't the detective warned her about Owen? He'd talked about a protection order and said he'd request a temporary one. He hadn't called or texted about that either. Her fingers crept to her cell. Should she send a quick text and ask?

Owen swaggered through the door. His gaze swept the conference room. His eyes narrowed as his anger targeted her. "What's she doing here?"

The sneer in his voice was as personal as the contempt in his expression.

"She's a beneficiary," Mr. Favero said. "Please take a seat."

Owen stormed to the end of the conference table. He slammed both palms on the shiny surface and leaned forward. "I told you she was stealing our money. Guess I was right, Ryan, wasn't I?"

"I didn't steal anything." Maddie knew she wasn't perfect, but *thief* wasn't part of her resume.

Owen's lip pulled back in a snarl and he shifted in her direction.

"Sit down." Ryan overrode whatever his brother planned to say. "Jeremy bailed your sorry ass out of jail so you could be here. Try to act like an adult."

"Fuck you." Owen took a step toward his older brother. "Don't give me that I'm-so-holy shit."

Another blonde-haired woman appeared at the door. "Oh lovely. Owen's being a jerk and Ryan is playing saint. Another fun family get-together."

"Fuck you too, Jess." Owen dropped into the chair beside Ryan's wife. No one had bothered to introduce her.

Jess glanced at Maddie, then took the seat opposite Owen, leaving a vacant seat next to Maddie.

She didn't nod, say hello or acknowledge Massie's presence. Fine. The more she saw of the Kaufman siblings, the less she liked any of them.

Long, silent minutes passed. The tension in the room left a bitter taste in Maddie's mouth. Periodically, everyone shifted in their seats and cast sideways glances at each other. Jess drummed her fingers on the table. Owen glared. Ryan seemed lost in thought. Maddie wondered if he was still processing the news about Daniel's cancer. Now that she thought about it, the cancer explained Daniel's recent pallor and fatigue. Had his children noticed? Had he waved away their concern the way he did hers?

Ryan's wife spoke to him in a low, urgent tone. He either didn't hear her or ignored her.

"Ryan." She jostled his arm.

He shook, as if waking from a bad dream. "What?"

"Time," she whispered.

He tapped his cell and checked the screen. "Where is he?"

"Probably asleep," Jess said.

"Where's Chris?" Ryan countered. He gave his sister an assessing look.

"You know he's at work. Jeremy's the one who needs to get his butt in here."

"I'll call him." Ryan pounded the cell phone's screen, annoyance visible on his face. Seconds later, the phone connected. "Where are you?" The belligerent tone made Maddie cringe.

Jeremy's answer thinned Ryan's lips. He punched the cell and re-pocketed it. "He's on his way."

Less than a minute later, the last of the Kaufman kids entered the conference room. The man, a thinner version of Daniel, with the wiry muscle of an outdoorsman, paused just inside the door. A smile twitched his mouth as he looked at the positions staked out around the table. "Ryan. Jess." He nodded at his brother and sister. Owen rated a long, cool inspection and thinned lips. "How was jail?"

A flush climbed Owen's cheeks and his glare shifted from his brother to Maddie. "More of *her* bullshit."

"Oh, she hit the security guard?" Jeremy crossed his arms and raised an eyebrow.

Owen puffed up his chest. "Don't start with me."

"Shut up, both of you." Ryan's voice wavered between resigned and belligerent.

"Gentlemen." Mr. Favero interceded. "Let's get started."

"Sure thing." Jeremy rounded the table, briefly touched a hand to his sister's shoulder, and dropped into the chair beside Maddie. He turned to her and offered his hand. "I'm Jeremy. You must be Madeline."

She nodded and shook his hand. The palm and fingers were hard and calloused, but the skin was as warm as his voice.

Well, at least one of Daniel's children didn't actively hate her.

Mr. Favero cleared his throat and centered a file folder in front of him. "I've been Daniel Kaufman's attorney for the past fifteen years. Daniel called me several weeks ago in order to make changes to his estate plan."

Maddie sensed rather than saw the unease ripple through the siblings. Did they think Daniel had completely changed his will? Left everything to her? That was so ridiculous she couldn't even fathom it. She'd rather see him every week, enjoying life, than using his money to make her life easier.

She cut her eyes and snuck a peak across the table. Owen, Ryan and his wife were all glaring at her. She didn't bother to look at Jess's expression. Beside her, Jeremy rested his hands on the table. His aura of calmness flowed over her. She took a breath, hoping to ease her tension.

"Daniel was of sound mind when he signed the new will. I will not attest to any evidence of coercion by any person or event."

"But if he was," Owen began.

"As I said, the decisions were Mr. Kaufman's. It is my responsibility to see that his wishes are carried out." The attorney cleared his throat. "The events surrounding Mr. Kaufman's death, however, are highly unusual. Until the case is settled, we cannot disburse any funds."

"What do you mean by 'settled'?" Jess demanded. "Until there's an arrest. A trial. What?"

The attorney ignored her question. "In addition, given the size of the estate, it will be subject to probate. Those proceedings are a matter of public record and another reason the Prosecuting Attorney has asked us to suspend submitting the will into record until the preliminary investigation is complete."

Local law enforcement had been briefed as to the beneficiaries of the estate.

"They knew before us?"

Maddie wasn't sure which of the brothers made that shocked comment. Instead, she processed bits and pieces of the previous days. If Daniel left her money, and apparently he did since she was invited to this fun party, no wonder the police were initially all over her. From their reaction today, the siblings clearly thought she'd made a grab for Daniel's money and had implied—at least she hoped it was merely implied— she'd killed him to get her hands on it. She'd never been so happy to have car trouble in her life. *Thank you Frank. You saved my butt in more ways than you know.*

"Your mother, of course, died several years ago and provisions were made in her will for various charitable contributions. Likewise, your father made several bequests." Mr. Favero listed half a dozen local charities which Maddie knew Daniel had supported during his lifetime.

"This week, Mr. Kaufman added a new bequest. To Madeline Larsson, one hundred thousand dollars."

Maddie gasped. In her wildest dreams, she'd thought maybe he'd leave her ten thousand dollars.

"Dad did *what*?" Jess demanded.

"Why does she get part of *our* money," Owen asked. "How much does he have anyway?"

The attorney continued. "An additional fifty thousand will be placed in a restricted account to pay for Ms Larsson's college education. A separate fifty thousand dollars will be placed in trust for her son, Caden Larsson, to fund his college education. If Caden has not entered college by the time he is aged twenty-five, the funds plus earnings will revert to the general estate."

Maddie stared at the attorney. Her hands covered her delighted smile. "Really? He left me money so I can finish college? And for my son?"

The attorney offered a brief smile before turning the page.

"Two hundred thousand?" Ryan's voice had an odd note to it. Maddie wasn't sure but it sounded like there was an unspoken, *Is that all?*

Two hundred thousand was more money than she could hope to accumulate in the foreseeable future. She was so happy it took her a moment to remember Ryan had thought Daniel had left most of his money to her. She tried to catch his eye, but he refused to look at her.

*Two hundred thousand.* Ryan stared straight ahead as he mouthed the words. He looked a little ill, which kinda pissed her off.

"To my children Ryan, Jessica and Jeremy, I leave my remaining estate, thirty three percent to each one. To my son Owen, I leave the remaining one percent and the advice to grow up. Owen spent his portion of my estate foolishly and frivolously in the years leading up to my death."

Owen erupted from his chair. It smashed into the wall, the crash reverberating in the shocked silence following Mr. Favero's statement. Hands slammed onto the table, he leaned toward the attorney. Spit flew from his lips. "You can't do that. You can't let him cut me out."

"It was Daniel's choice."

"And you. You bitch. Why do you get money when I don't?" Owen kicked the chair out of his way. It slammed against the wall again, leaving a long gouge.

"Mr. Kaufman." The attorney half-rose. "Control yourself."

Maddie gasped. She didn't know what to say that wouldn't make things worse. Part of her wanted to throw the money back in his face, but dammit, that wasn't what Daniel wanted. She never asked him to give her anything. He recognized the gift would make a huge difference in her life. So to hell with all of them and their nasty little minds.

Owen stomped around the end of the table. "We all suspected you were a gold-digging slut. This proves it."

Jeremy stood, blocking Owen's path. "Sit down. You're not helping."

"Get out of my way, asshole. Dad always thought you and Ryan were such fucking saints, but we know better, don't we?"

"Shut up Owen. Sit down. We aren't the ones who constantly hit Dad up for money." Ryan jumped into the middle. "We weren't the ones who hit him. You want to throw around some accusations? Let's put the rest of the cards on the table. Tell the family whether you shot Dad."

# CHAPTER SIXTEEN

*Tuesday mid-morning*

JC called Nunez as he drove into Pasco from the airport. "Can you help me with a couple of interviews?"

Nunez hesitated.

"Look, I know you've got your own work, but I need to get to all four of these guys *today.* If there is a woman, I have to have her name. If there isn't one, I got two assholes to haul into the station."

"Just two?" Nunez chuckled and JC knew he had him.

"At least two. Look, all of these guys work for Ryan. If Chris tells his brother I know about that 04:00 car ride, Ryan could put pressure on his employees to back his story."

"Payback's gonna be a bitch," Nunez warned.

"Isn't it always?" A call waiting beeped. "Hang on a second."

"I got something." The voice was young and excited. The number was blocked.

"Who is this?"

"Dickerman. Pasco PD."

JC remembered the kid from an earlier case. Young. Eager to prove himself. Cocky to cover his lack of experience.

"Whacha got?" He glanced at his watch and wondered what time the salesmen had to be at the dealership.

"Coveralls. Bloody coveralls." A triumphant note sounded in Dickerman's voice.

*Yes.* If he'd had a free hand, he'd have given a victory pump. "Hang on." JC switched back to Nunez. "Can you take these two?" He rattled off the names and then clicked over to Dickerman. "You know where the crime lab is?"

"Franklin sheriff's?" The young officer was practically hyperventilating with excitement.

"Yeah. Meet me there. And slow down. Let's make sure we have the chain of evidence nailed down." JC flipped a U-turn and headed for the lab, hoping he was making the right call.

Fifteen minutes later, JC and Dickerman logged the coveralls into evidence.

"Good work. We suspected the killer wore protective clothing when he moved the body and the car."

"We've been checking every trash receptacle between the crime scene and town. I didn't think we'd ever clear all those businesses on Stearman." Dickerman shook his head and folded his arms. "We worked down to the golf course. There's a dumpster out front next to the parking lot, but there's another one hidden on the back nine. That's where I found it."

JC tapped around on his phone and brought up a map of the area. "Straight down 4th, then over to the golf course."

The golf course was the center of the

overlapping circles. Each sibling's residence and workplace. And a probably bogus romantic rendezvous point. He studied the route Ryan supposedly took to meet Chris. Did any of that actually happen?

If Ryan had dumped his father's car and body north of town, the golf course made a convenient place to get rid of evidence. For that matter, Chris could've stashed a car at either the golf course or one of the businesses near the railroad and driven back to wherever he met his father and left his truck. Hell, Jeremy could've played a part in the murder or cover-up too. He'd admitted he didn't have an alibi for at least part of the night. And Owen. JC grimaced. Owen could've dragged any of the others into bailing him out.

Except if Chris wasn't taking Ryan back to the dealership—whatever he'd been doing at the golf course—then there was no reason for him to be traveling north on 20th.

Too many questions. Not enough answers. He stashed the phone in his pocket. "How fast can we get the blood analyzed? A blood type?"

"That'll be quick." The tech reached for the bag. "DNA will take longer."

"Wait." JC pulled on gloves and opened the bag. He held up the coveralls by the shoulders. "What size is this?"

Coveralls were based on chest size and height rather than waist size like jeans or overalls.

The tech poked at the collar. "A 40 Regular."

JC studied the garment, gauging sizes. The coveralls wouldn't fit him. Too short and too small through the shoulders. Jeremy was his height and

Chris an inch shorter. Both would be too tall to get into the garment. Chris was also at least a size 44, maybe a 46, with a stockier build than Jeremy.

Ryan or Owen though...

"No company or individual name." Dickerman pointed at the chest pocket.

"Could've gotten them anywhere." All four of the men—the Kaufmans and Chris—had easy access to protective clothing through their jobs. But wouldn't those coveralls be branded with a company logo? JC refolded the garment and handed it to the tech. "We need DNA on both the blood and the sweat. Let's see if it'll tell us who was wearing this."

"You got reference samples we can match?" she asked.

"I will soon." He suspected Chris and Jeremy would willingly provide test samples. Even if it cleared them specifically—which by now he suspected it would—Jeremy's results would give him mitochondrial DNA. That would be enough to tell if the subject DNA came from the same mother. To get a warrant for the other men's DNA, he needed more evidence. He turned to Dickerman. "This could be a huge break. Good work."

The kid swelled with pride.

It could also be a complete bust if the coveralls belonged to a groundskeeper who'd cut himself on a trimmer. "Now we need to find the weapon."

Dickerman all but saluted. "I'm on it."

JC hoped the pistol was found—or was at the bottom of the Columbia River—and not where it could be used on another victim.

"Ryan? Cheating on Emily? No way."

"You sure?" After his detour at the crime lab, JC had caught Manan at home and met Travis at a coffee shop downtown.

"Positive. The guy isn't the type." Travis' hand slashed, cutting off the possibility. "He loves his wife and kids. He'd never do anything to jeopardize that."

Manan had said the same thing. "I heard he met a woman last Thursday after you finished setting up for that sales event."

Travis shook his head. "Somebody's feeding you a load of bullshit. Ryan didn't meet a woman that night. His dad was pulling into the parking lot when I left."

"His dad?" JC went very still inside. *No assumptions. No tunnel vision.* Daniel could've talked to his son and left.

"Yeah. Some asshole probably saw the car and made an assumption based on their own dirty mind."

"Assumed it was a hookup."

"And you know what they say about assumptions." Travis picked up his coffee and polished off the last inch.

JC nodded. "Ryan's dad stop by the dealership often?"

"Not really. He brings his Lexus in—routine maintenance, oil changes. Ryan takes care of it for him, so I know the car."

"Kinda late to be doing a service drop off."

"His old man's a night owl. Although..." Travis rubbed his jaw. "I don't remember seeing his car over the weekend. With the chaos of our sales event, I could've missed it."

"Anything unusual happen recently at the dealership?"

"Nah. That event got the big bosses off our ass though. It's been a slow fall. Nobody was buying. Guess we were all waiting to see what the economy would do." Travis shrugged. "Ryan's been wound pretty tight. Guess they chew on him more than us. We kinda hoped he'd lighten up after this weekend." He stopped and did a mental rewind. "Shit. Ryan's dad was killed this weekend. No wonder he looks like he's falling apart."

"It's hardest on the kids."

"That's why you're here. Man..." Travis rotated the empty cup between his palms.

"I'm surprised Ryan's working. I guess with your event going on..." JC left it dangling.

"Ryan was in and out all weekend, keeping things moving. He looked like he was ready to hurl most of the time, but he handles the back office part. Approves the sales details. But if you're asking, between all of us, we should be able to alibi him for most of the weekend."

"I'm sure he'll appreciate that." Except it wasn't the weekend Ryan needed to explain. "Is there a way to check whether Kaufman's Lexus came in for service that night? When you saw his dad?"

Travis hesitated and JC wondered if the guy was considering whether the information helped or hurt his boss.

"We're still tracing Daniel Kaufman's movements. Anything you can add to the timeline will help the family."

"Talk to Leslie." Travis crushed the cup and rose. "She keeps the service log. It's in there, even

145

when we comp it. Ryan would've paid for any parts and that'd be on the register too."

To JC's relief, Ryan wasn't at the dealership when he stopped to chat with Leslie. The dealership was quiet with the after lunch lull. Only random equipment noises drifted in from the service area.

"Ryan isn't here right now? Something about a meeting with the attorney?" She had one of those voices that made everything a question.

He remembered the meeting with the attorney was scheduled for that day. So much had happened, it felt like a week should've passed. Seven days instead of seven hours since he'd listened to Chris' story about a girl. "I'll catch up with him later. Can you tell me if his dad dropped off his car for service last week?" It was possible Daniel had dropped the car at the dealership and met someone other than his son afterward.

Except that didn't mesh with the Lexus and Daniel's body ending up miles away at a closed business.

She tapped around on the computer a while. "The last time his car was in for service was this summer? In August?"

"Thanks." Another piece of the puzzle. He could tentatively place Daniel and his Lexus at the dealership. Now to prove it. He took a step away from the counter, then stopped. "One last question. What color are your service techs' coveralls?"

"Their coveralls?" This time the question was

accompanied by puzzled eyebrows. "Grey?"

Just like the ones Dickerman found. Still not remotely conclusive. "Thanks. Just curious. Do they come in with your company logo already on them?"

She shook her head. "We have someone local? They make the name patches for the employees? Attach everything?"

"So you can order the uniforms in bulk?"

"It's less expensive?"

He found a smile and left. *Not if that pair of coveralls came from the dealership.* That would prove extremely "expensive" for both Ryan and Daniel.

JC had nearly made it to the unmarked when his cell buzzed. He glanced at the screen, a courthouse extension. "Dimitrak."

"That protection order you requested came through. You going to serve it or should we call the woman and let her know how to proceed?"

Damn. With the investigation breaking open, he hadn't called Madeline. He walked a little faster and unlocked the car. The jail was connected to the courthouse and shared security with it. "What's Owen Kaufman's status?"

"Hold on."

He settled behind the wheel. A few moments later, the deputy came back. "Kaufman was bailed out this morning."

"We had an agreement to hold him." JC banged a fist into the steering wheel.

"Don't shoot me. Apparently somebody got an attorney involved and got him released."

Damn. Damn. Damn. Owen might or might not be the shooter but he was an explosion ready to go off at the smallest provocation.

"Tell the deputies to keep as close an eye on him as we can." He clicked off and called the sheriff's department. "Send an APB to Pasco, Richland, Kennewick and Benton County for Owen Kaufman. I want to know if he so much as scratches his ass. Second, I'm headed to the courthouse with warrants for every security camera around Ryan Kaufman's dealership for Thursday night and Friday morning. How much overtime has the sheriff authorized?"

Maddie didn't tell her mother about Daniel's gift when she dropped off Caden Tuesday evening. Explaining would take too long and she was still processing it herself. Fortunately her first rotation at the casino was the poker tables. While the game was more complicated for the players, for the dealer, the pace was slower than the rapid fire of blackjack. At those stations, the casino wanted to turn over as many rounds as possible. Blackjack depended upon a high volume of small bets.

The higher betting limits at the poker table usually meant larger tips for the dealers, so it was a preferred position. Apparently she wasn't on management's shit-list over the mess with Owen.

Thanks to Daniel's generous gift, however, financial concern wouldn't be a constant refrain for her life. A smile curved her lips. Happiness added an extra flourish as she slid chips around at the end of the hand. One of the players met her gaze and tossed a chip her way. "Always fun to see a pretty lady happy."

"I am happy tonight." She caught the chip,

laughed, and spun a new round of cards. While her hands handled cards, chips and bets, her mind raced. The attorney said the estate wouldn't pay out for a while, but she planned to quit her second job this week. More sleep and more time with Caden were completely worth the temporary cash crunch.

Owen was the only fly in her universe. Her smile faltered before she remembered to keep it intact.

Would Owen really do something stupid because he was mad at his father?

At her first break, Maddie called Detective Dimitrak to ask about the restraining order. Had the judge granted the detective's request? If so, was there an exception clause to a protection order? Her immediate question was the funeral. The service was scheduled for Friday morning. As much as she wanted to pay her final respects to Daniel, if it was a choice of Owen or her attending, it was only right that Owen be allowed to go to his father's funeral.

If the judge didn't grant the restraining order, she'd go. If there was an order in place, she'd stay away.

It was the other possible places she could encounter Owen that worried her.

A man answered the phone at the sheriff's department. "Detective Dimitrak is out in the field. I'll leave a message that you called."

Frank Phalen caught her as she left the dealer's room. "Your car will be ready by Friday."

"Oh, thank goodness. My mother will be so happy to get *her* car back. She really needs it and I was afraid I might have to rent one." Maddie fell into step beside him as they headed to the gaming floor. "What was wrong with my car and how much is it going to cost me?"

"The starter had gone bad. That's what's taking so long. They had to order the part. They went ahead and serviced it—cleaned the injectors—while they had it." Frank gave her a disapproving frown. "It was long overdue."

She shrugged and raised her hands. "I changed the oil."

"You might want to check the owner's manual for the rest of the maintenance. My guy said he could bring it over here. Maybe your mom can drop you off and you can drive it home."

"I'm going to Daniel Kaufman's funeral on Friday morning. Do you know what time he plans to bring it by?"

They talked through the logistics. "I tell you what. If your mom can drop you at the church, I'll bring the car over there and we can ride back here."

"I hate to make you go out of your way."

"Not a problem. Have a good night." Frank tossed a casual salute and headed into the office area.

Maddie watched him leave. For a moment she wondered why Detective Dimitrak and the security chief disliked each other so much. She shrugged and headed for her station. It was undoubtedly a guy thing.

Although she checked her phone at every break, the detective's text message didn't arrive until nearly midnight. It included his cell phone number. She tapped in the number.

"Dimitrak."

"Hi. This is Madeline Larsson." She glanced around the dealer's room and edged closer to the lockers. "I was wondering about the protection order for Owen Kaufman?"

He sighed. "I meant to call you earlier. A lot's going on. The judge granted the order but Owen hasn't been served. He was bailed out this morning and I haven't had a chance to track him down."

"He was at the attorney's office this afternoon when Mr. Favero told us about the will."

"How'd that go?"

A smile creased her face. She told him about the attorney meeting—and the will's surprising contents. Then she told him the rest. "Owen slammed out of the office, yelling and ranting."

"Not happy about the way the will turned out."

"That's an understatement. He blames me for everything instead of accepting it's his own fault. Jeremy walked me to my car to make sure Owen didn't do anything stupid. Well, more stupid than the other things he's done." She didn't tell the detective the last part, but the hardest looking of the Kaufman clan had been the kindest. Jeremy had also asked her to have coffee with him after the meeting, but she'd explained about her class and regretfully declined.

"Good. You need to watch out for Owen. I can have the order served on him tomorrow. One of the deputies can track him down."

"Well, I was wondering about the funeral." She told him about the probability they would both want to attend.

"You're sure you want to go?"

"I think I should."

There was a pause and Maddie cast another quick glance at the other dealers in the room. None seemed to be paying attention to her.

"I tell you what," the detective said. "I plan to

attend the funeral too. If you're okay until then, I can bring the order and serve Owen at the end of the service. It doesn't go into effect until he's served. That way he wouldn't be in violation if you're both there."

She nodded, although he couldn't see it. "I can stay mostly out of sight until then."

"Call if you need help." He ended the call.

Maddie tucked her phone back into her locker. She could handle Owen—maybe—with help from another source. She was meeting Jeremy after she finished work tomorrow afternoon—her last day at her second job.

She didn't tell JC that either.

# CHAPTER SEVENTEEN

JC drove himself—and as many deputies as he could get his hands on—around the clock. He pounded paperwork, requesting phone records, search warrants, pulling together bits and pieces of Daniel, Owen and Ryan's movements during the critical days. Through it all, he struggled to keep a lid on the investigation, to not tip either the press or the Kaufman siblings about the direction of the investigation.

Teams of deputies and uniformed Pasco officers armed with search warrants fanned out across the city. On Wednesday, every security camera from the streets around the dealership was hit with a warrant for its records on the night of the murder. Throughout the following day, digital copies of security tapes fed into the sheriff's department, where other officers poured over the feeds, searching for Daniel, his children, his car, and his children's cars.

By Thursday morning, they had Daniel's Lexus arriving at the dealership at 00:17 with one passenger and leaving at 01:24 with two. The angle and crummy resolution didn't give a clear enough picture to identify either person. They couldn't even tell who was driving or if both people were alive. They had a blurred photo of the car approaching the Highway 395 entrance at 01:27. The vehicle vanished after that.

Someone drove the car up Highway 395, most likely to I-182, then exited the Interstate at 4th Avenue. Roughly five miles, less than ten minutes by car, but it would mean a two-hour walk back to the dealership.

Another round of warrants flooded the businesses between 4th Avenue and the dumpsite, but those buildings were far removed from the street. Their cameras focused on doors and parking lots. The Lexus and its occupants passed by them unseen.

Other results trickled in. Phone records showed a call to the victim's cell phone from a fast food place near the dealership at 21:46 on Thursday night. The teenager working the shift picked Ryan out of a photo array.

The lab called: "The blood type from the bloody coveralls matched Daniel Kaufman's type. You get those DNA samples from the family?"

"Working on it."

DNA matching for the blood—and the sweat—would take weeks, but the story was coming together. The victim went to the dealership on Thursday night to meet someone, most likely Ryan. He may or may not have ridden away still breathing.

But in spite of the mounting circumstantial evidence, JC didn't have enough.

He stared at the white boards, the files, the stacks of records. Taken individually, each item he'd uncovered could be explained away. Alternative scenario? *My dad left after we talked at the dealership. No idea who was with him or where they went.* The phone call from the fast food place? *My cell battery died. Do you have any idea how hard it is to find a pay phone in this town?*

Only the woman—who still hadn't been uncovered—could trip up Ryan.

He had circumstantial evidence implicating the guy. He needed tangible evidence that the PA could put in front of a jury and convince them Ryan pulled the trigger.

JC laid out forms and began to carefully construct a reality. One that might let him uncover the piece of evidence that Ryan—or his attorney—couldn't brush away.

This is it.

JC walked into the judge's chamber early Friday morning, delivering a request for a coordinated search of Ryan's workplace, home and car. For long moments, there was silence as the judge read and flipped pages.

Finally he looked up. "You think this man murdered his father?" The judge looked again at the paperwork.

"Yes sir. Unfortunately, I do."

The judge looked at JC, frowned, and then scrawled a signature on the warrant. "Don't make me regret this. People want this crime solved. They don't like it when solid citizens get shot. But they like it less when a solid citizen is falsely accused."

"We're working hard to solve it." JC kept his thoughts about solid citizens to himself. He picked up the signed paperwork and left the courthouse. He had his cell phone to his ear before he cleared security. "We're a go. We'll take the dealership. Team two to the house."

The teams rallied in a parking lot near the dealership. Priorities reviewed, JC's squad streamed through the office doors. The forensic group concentrated on the employee locker room, while JC started on Ryan's office. Five minutes later, he reached into the center desk draw and snagged a brown pill bottle. A savage grin spread across his face. "Well, well, well. Got you, asshole."

The deputy across the room looked up. "Whacha got?"

"Premeditation." JC shook the pill vial. "Phenobarbital. Filled Thursday morning. A script for Ryan Kaufman."

"The vic wasn't drugged." Confusion knotted the deputy's forehead.

"Nope. And somehow I don't think Ryan's taking sleeping pills at work." Ryan had filled the prescription the day before his father was murdered. The day after he found out his dad was cutting people out of his will. "I bet I know who *was* taking them."

He glanced at his watch. Time to move. He stepped across the office area and found the duty officer. "I'm headed to the funeral. Ryan's car will be there. I need one of the techs with me."

The officer noted the time and departure on his sheet. "Take Hernandez. Abetya and Lewis just found blood trace in the locker room."

JC's hand tightened around the bagged pill bottle. "The son of a bitch did it. Killed his father, cleaned himself up here, and then went home like nothing happened."

"If there's blood in the asshole's car—"

"Or a pistol," JC interjected.

"—Hernandez will find it."

# CHAPTER EIGHTEEN

*Friday*

JC planted his feet and widened his stance. From his position at the back of the church he could watch the assembled group. The Kaufman family sat in the front pew. There were a few new faces among the black-clad mourners. One of Daniel's brothers and his wife had driven over from Boise. Another sister came from Seattle. Owen sat at the end of the row. JC fingered the restraining order. He'd serve it, then hit Ryan for his car keys and cheek swab.

He swept another circuit of the church. Logistics shouldn't be a problem. The main exits were behind him at the head of the aisles. Doorways on either side of the pulpit area led to the office corridor and another exit. He'd stationed a uniformed officer there in case Ryan—or Owen—made a run for it. The case against Ryan wasn't 100% airtight. They had Ryan coming back from the dumpsite, but it was still possible Owen had killed their father and gone running to his big brother to clean up his mess.

The rest of the church looked pretty much like he expected. Flowers and a framed picture of Daniel Kaufman surrounded a gleaming wood pillar, which held an urn.

The family had cremated Kaufman. JC wondered if it was at Daniel's request or if they couldn't bear the thought of looking at what was left of their dad.

Another song rolled out of the speakers, one of those praise-worship ones that JC didn't recognize. The church was nearly full. Older people, probably friends from Kaufman's working days at the Labs, had shown up. He recognized several neighbors. Others were church members he'd seen or talked with earlier in the week. Madeline Larsson sat alone in a side pew. He'd noticed Jeremy Kaufman walk over to greet her when she arrived. A small smile tugged at his mouth. You go, Jeremy.

Or should he say, go Maddie?

The service was short. A few hymns. The preacher and a couple of older people spoke. None of Daniel's children offered a eulogy. Another hymn and then the crowd was on the move. Ryan picked up the urn and started up the right side aisle. His brothers and sister flanked him and the rest of the family trailed behind in a ragged honor guard.

Time to move.


Maddie scanned the parking lot and peered up and down the street. No Civic. No Frank. She tapped her phone to check the time. The service was shorter than she'd expected, but Frank had said he was coming.

Shivering, she pulled her jacket closer. The wind held the beginning of winter's bite. She noticed Owen talking to the detective. Or rather arguing with him. Owen looked seriously pissed. She inched back from the pavement. No sense in making herself an easy target.

"Problem?"

She jumped, nearly dropping her phone. Swinging around, she found Daniel's oldest son beside her. "No, no problem."

Why did he fluster her?

Her well-honed creep detector pinged a warning, but Ryan hadn't been overtly hostile the way his younger brother had.

"My car...Frank...he's delivering it. It's not here."

Ryan adjusted the urn in the crook of his arm. "We're heading to the cemetery to place Dad's ashes. Why don't you ride with me? I can drop you off after. Since it's Friday, I'm guessing you have to work tonight."

"That's okay. I mean, thanks. But...I'd hate for you to go out of your way." She shot another glance at the street. Where was Frank? "And isn't that, the cemetery part, just for your family?"

"Look, I'm sorry about the way we've acted. Dad liked you. He'd want you to be there."

Way to layer on the guilt. But it was about Daniel, not her.

He pulled car keys from his pocket. "Come on."

She gave him a weak smile. "Sure."

Trailing Ryan to his car, her fingers flew across her cell phone screen. To Frank: *"Where are you?"*

Ugh, she couldn't send that. Delete delete delete. "The funeral's over. I'm going to the cemetery with Ryan."

Small pulsing dots signaled a response. "Pasco

City View? I'll bring the car out there."

"Thanks." She wasn't sure if it was for bringing the car or if it was for rescuing her from Ryan. She stashed her phone in her pocket and climbed into the car.

JC served the restraining order first. He slapped the papers into Owen's hand. "Stay away from Madeline Larsson unless you want to go back to jail."

Owen reacted with typical outrage. "Me?" His fist crumpled the papers. "Why the fuck is this my fault? If she hadn't made a play for my father, he'd still be alive—"

"Do you know something about Daniel Kaufman's murder that you haven't told me?"

"No." He blinked mid-rant.

"Any evidence to back your claim?"

A flush climbed Owen's neck and cheeks. "I know she was involved. I can't prove it, but why else would he leave her that kind of money?"

"Because he respected hard work and a hard worker?" *Something you need to learn how to do.*

Owen threw the papers on the sidewalk and stomped on them. "Fuck this and fuck you."

"You might want to use that college fund your dad left you. Go to school and learn some new words."

With a one-finger salute, Owen turned and stormed to a new Ford F-150. He laid rubber on the parking lot pavement.

JC watched him leave. *Asshole.* He'd find him later and get a DNA sample. He sorta hoped he could charge him for something. With a sigh, he scanned the parking area, spotted Emily and Jess, and strolled over to the women. Next on the list… "Glad I caught you together."

They turned and gave him mildly puzzled expressions.

"I know this is a serious occasion and I'm truly sorry about Daniel. But I do have a question."

"Okay," Emily's voice held a cautious note.

"I've been running around to places your husbands and brothers work. And wow, they really jump in and get their hands dirty." He paused and rubbed his chin. "Chris and Jeremy both wear uniforms. Do you have to wash those things?"

Jess snorted a laugh and then glanced around to see if anyone noticed. "A commercial cleaning service does that, thank goodness. Chris brings home enough grease that he's still a pain."

"Guess you're the only one who doesn't have that challenge." JC smiled at Emily.

"Not so fast." Emily held up a hand. "Ryan manages to get car junk on himself on a regular basis. He actually leaves a set of clothes at the dealership so he can change."

"Smart thinking." The deputies hadn't found spare clothes in Ryan's office or the employee locker room. So that was how he did it. Showered and changed clothes to get rid of trace evidence. They'd recovered blood in the locker room. The clothes—including the shoes—were probably in the Columbia River along with the gun. They'd never find them.

They chatted a few moments, then JC said, "If you'll excuse us, Jessica, I need to talk with Emily for a second."

"Sure. Em, we're heading over to the cemetery in a few minutes."

"I'll be there in a second."

JC couldn't hit Emily with a search warrant. He couldn't force her to testify against her husband. She'd have to want to cooperate. "This may sound like a strange question, but are either you or Ryan having a hard time sleeping?"

The easy smile left her face. "We're upset about Daniel, but no, not really."

"What about before Daniel died?"

"Why are you asking me this?" Suspicion had her inching away.

"That first time we talked, you said you 'slept like a log' the night Daniel was killed. You commented on how unusual that was for you."

"So?"

If Ryan had drugged her, a truck could've driven through the house and she wouldn't have known it. He took a deep breath. "It's possible you were given a sleeping pill that night. Would you be willing to take a drug test?"

"You think I'm using drugs?" Outrage colored both her voice and her cheeks.

"No, nothing like that." He reached out a placating hand. "I don't think you knew about it."

Her eyes narrowed as she connected the dots. "I didn't…You think Ryan…? No way. He wouldn't." Understanding heightened her flush. "He didn't have anything to do with Daniel's death." She pulled out her phone and tapped around. "He'll tell you."

"Ryan would want to protect you. If he wanted to keep you completely out of the way, wouldn't you rather know instead of always wondering?"

"Dammit." Her lips thinned as the phone pressed her ear. "Where are you? Call me when you get this message."

JC scanned the parking lot but didn't see Ryan or his car.

Emily's hand lowered and her lip trembled as if she were fighting tears.

"It'll only take a minute." *Careful, don't push too hard.*

"He couldn't," she whispered. "Why would you say that?"

"If nothing shows up, won't that help? Erase any doubt? Your sleeping so deep could be a fluke. That's all." *Don't think too hard. Don't focus on the big question. Not yet. Just do this one little thing.*

For a long moment, she stood lost in thought.

He kept his voice gentle. "Don't you want to know?"

Finally she sighed. "What do I have to do?"


Ryan turned right onto Court Street. Maddie watched a series of low-slung strip malls and block apartment buildings flow past her window. Her stomach rumbled as they passed a taco truck. She tightened her arms across her middle and hoped Ryan hadn't heard.

His phone chirped, breaking the uncomfortable silence. He tugged it out, glanced at the screen, and sent the call to voice mail.

"Are you sure your wife didn't want to ride with you?" He'd hustled her into the car before she'd registered his wife's absence.

"She was planning something with Jess. They'll ride together."

Time stretched. Maddie eyed the urn. Ryan had propped it at a precarious angle on the console. Should she move it? Or would he consider it more intrusion into family matters?

He powered onto the interstate and swept across the bridge over the railroad that cut through the city. A minute later, he looped around the exit ramp and headed south again into the eastern section of Pasco.

"Well." Ryan broke the silence. "Apparently you like Kaufman men."

"Excuse me?" She gave him a total double-take. He'd apologized earlier for being a jerk. Guess that was out the window. And what was that comment supposed to mean?

"Dad's gone. Jeremy's rich now. Don't think we didn't notice."

"You think… That is so offensive, it…it... That's why you offered me a ride. Forget it. Pull over and let me out."

"Don't be stupid. Nice try, but you made yourself a part of this."

"I'm not a part of anything. How many times do I have to say this? I didn't do anything except be nice to your dad. From everything I've seen, you're the one obsessed with money. I was doing just fine, paying for college and living my life before your dad left me some money. Which he did out of the kindness of his heart. And newsflash. It was your dad's money, not yours. Funny how your family conveniently forgets that part."

Ryan whipped into the cemetery parking lot. "This was a mistake."

"No kidding." She released the seat belt and reached for her purse. Her elbow connected with the urn. It teetered and rattled. She reached for it at the same moment Ryan did. Hands scrambling, they watched as the lid did a slow motion bounce off the dashboard. The urn toppled and tumbled and the ashes cascaded onto the floorboard.

"Oh. My. God." She gave Ryan a horrified glance and picked up the urn base. Should she scoop up the ashes? Her hands hovered above the pile. This wasn't like a campfire or cleaning up some mess Caden made. This was a person.

Used to be a person.

A hint of blue peeked through the grainy ashes. "What…?" She nudged at the speck with her toe and a poker chip emerged. "Daniel's lucky chip. You found it. The police said they were looking for it." Her words petered out as realization sunk in. Daniel had the chip at the casino. It vanished the night he was murdered. The only way Ryan could've ended up with it was if Ryan met with him that night…which made Ryan either the killer or an accomplice.

She stared at the blue circle. There was no way his brothers or sister would've ever looked at the ashes in the urn. Who did that unless they planned to sprinkle the ashes? With the memorial niche, what were the odds the chip would've ever seen the light of day?

As if from a distance, she turned and, mouth open, stared at Ryan. No words emerged. This could not be happening. He looked like a choirboy, not a cold-blooded killer. Like a smooth card-counter, Ryan had hidden behind the more obvious suspect, his volatile brother Owen.

"Why couldn't you get arrested like you were supposed to?"

Oh shit. He really did kill Daniel.

Ryan fumbled under his seat. "You have got to be the unluckiest person in the world."

She tugged at the door. The lock released and the door swung open. She lunged for freedom.

"Not so fast,"

She turned back to Ryan and stared straight into the business end of a pistol.

After handing Emily off to Hernandez—no way was he giving her time to reconsider volunteering a urine sample—JC went looking for the next Kaufman on his list.

If Ryan confronted his father that night, he could've planned the murder or he might've panicked mid-stream and pulled the trigger. Drugging his wife reeked of premeditation. Either way, by dumping the car and body in a remote location, he'd needed a way back to the dealership where his own car was parked. The five-mile, less than ten-minute drive would've turned into a two-hour walk.

But why would he call Chris instead of his brother? Ryan had made a point about being closer to Jeremy than he was to Owen. Chris hadn't even been mentioned.

Unless...

JC caught Jeremy as he unlocked his Toyota. "What time did Ryan call?"

A sardonic smile flitted over his face, as if he'd been waiting for JC to ask that question. "Started about three. I was working that hydraulic job and ignored his first calls. Finally answered a little before four."

"What did he say?"

Jeremy leaned against the pickup truck. "He had some bullshit story about a woman. My brother is a lot of things, but I don't think cheating on his wife is one of his flaws."

"So he called you in the middle of the night to talk about a woman."

Another smile turned up the corners of Jeremy's mouth. "He wanted me to come pick him up. Said she'd left his ass on the side of the road. I told him to start walking. If he was dumb enough to get himself into a mess, he could get himself out."

"You think there was a woman?"

Jeremy stayed quiet for a long moment, then sighed. "It's better than the alternative, isn't it?"

"Where is he?"

"He left about five minutes ago, headed to the mausoleum." Jeremy straightened abruptly and his lips thinned. "He has Maddie with him."

"With him?"

"In his car." He nodded at a cluster of people near the front door of the church. "I saw Owen take off. Emily is over there with Jess and Chris. Only the six of us were supposed to go place Dad's ashes."

JC turned and sprinted for his car. If the family blamed Madeline for their father's death, separating her from the crowd could be deadly.


"You stupid bitch. If you'd left it alone, it would've

been buried with him."

She pressed her purse to her chest as if the leather created a shield. Under her hands, her heart thundered a frantic race. Run, her brain shrieked. Freeze, her muscles ordered.

"Get in the car." He twitched the gun.

Every horror flick she'd ever seen flashed through her mind. All of them started with the girl getting into the car.

*Don't get into the car.*

"Now I have to go to Plan B, which was supposed to be Plan A."

"Or you can let me leave."

"Nope. See, you tried to attack me because I found Dad's tournament chip in your possession." He tilted his head at the car where the blue disc lay buried in Daniel's ashes. "I wrestled the gun away but unfortunately you got shot in the process."

"That plan doesn't really work for me." Her gaze darted over the flat landscape. Small trees, too little to hide behind. No fences. The mausoleum loomed in front of her, the door beckoning.

Don't do it. For all she knew that door was the only way in—or out. She'd be trapped inside with nowhere to hide or run.

"Move it." Ryan poked the pistol at her again.

Please God, don't let him jerk the trigger while he's waving the gun around.

The snap of flags caught her attention. The flags rippled in the breeze, marking the graves of fallen heroes. She could use a hero right now. The longs rows of headstones beyond them snagged her gaze. They offered a hiding place.

"Do you want me to shoot you right here?"

"Like later would be better?" She sprinted toward the closest available cover—the cluster of bushes surrounding a large tombstone.

"Get back here." Ryan's yell was nearly incoherent with rage.

A bang like a car backfiring sounded. Maddie swore she felt something whiz past her head. She zigged and zagged. Somewhere she'd read it was harder to hit a running, dodging target.

Ryan's footsteps pounded on the ground behind her. "Stop. I swear to God I'll shoot you."

He was gaining on her. She gave up the zigzag, sprinted and dove behind a large cross. Scrambling on her hands and knees, she crawled to the next headstone.

He flailed at the bushes.

She squirmed deeper into the hedge. Now what? She had to stall and pray Frank or Ryan's brothers showed up. Someone who could talk some sense into him. Yeah, and what if Ryan shot her before anyone else arrived?

She fingered her phone and tapped 911.

"911, what is your emergency?"

"I'm at City View Cemetery. Ryan Kaufman is shooting at me." She cupped her hand around the phone, praying Ryan wouldn't hear her.

"Stay on the line. An officer is en route."

Where was Ryan? The operator was still talking but she crammed the phone in her pocket and hoped the operator could hear. She peered over the top of the marker. Ryan was at the opposite side of the group of headstones, poking the gun into the bushes and peering into the openings he created. "Why are you doing this?"

170

His head jerked. He whipped the pistol free and pointed it at her.

Damn. I should've kept my mouth shut.

"This whole fucking disastrous week is your fault."

"My fault?"

"You targeted our dad. You thought you were going to get everything—"

"I didn't target anybody and I sure didn't know he planned to leave me anything. I didn't even know he was sick."

"Shut up." He stepped to the right around the circle of headstones with the pistol leading the way. "If you'd stayed out of this, none of it would've happened."

"All of it would have happened. Your dad was sick. Not just sick. He was dying. He chose not to tell you because he was protecting you." She scooted to the left, ducking from headstone to headstone. Maybe if she could keep him talking he wouldn't shoot her.

"You think I don't know that now? Why didn't he tell me?" Two sharp bangs sounded and chips of marble flew from the monument she'd been tucked behind.

A shriek filled her throat but she bit it back. She had to stay calm and not panic. Staying in control meant maybe she'd survive. She had to live through this for her son. "Did you talk to Daniel about it?"

"Of course I did," he shouted. "I asked him point blank. 'Owen said you changed your will. Did you?' He looked at me like I was some blood-sucking pond scum and said 'yes.' And I…I…"

"You what?" She wasn't sure if the sirens in the

171

distance were real or her imagination. Hurry.

Another bullet ripped through the shrubbery and pinged off a tombstone. A chip slashed her cheek and she gasped. Blood trickled down her cheek.

"Owen went crazy. He started yelling and then he had this damn pistol and everything went to hell. Then my fuck-up of a brother left me holding the bag like he always does."

"Owen shot him?"

"Yes!" More bullets sprayed around her. "What was I supposed to do? Turn in my brother? It wouldn't bring Dad back."

She prayed the 911 operator heard his confession. And that it was enough to convict both brothers. "Why'd you take Daniel's chip, Ryan?"

"Don't call him 'Daniel.' He's Mr. Kaufman to you."

"Why'd you take the chip?"

"Because he always had it with him. If that damned security guard hadn't been mooning around you, I'd have planted the chip in your car. Hell, I could've put the gun under the seat."

The gun he was firing at her now? "Put the gun down, Ryan. You'll never get away with killing me."

"We got away with it before." His voice had changed again, taking on the icy tone Asher's did when he was stone-cold sober—and planning to hurt her anyway, just because he could.


JC tore out of the church parking lot, the bubble light blinking from the roof. He hit the speed dial for Dispatch. "Officer requesting backup. City View cemetery." He gave them Ryan's car and tag. "Assume he's armed."

Dispatch acknowledged.

His cell buzzed. Dickerman.

"I was at the dealership this morning."

"Yeah?" JC blew past a low-rider pickup truck.

"Short version. Owen Kaufman is driving a dealership truck."

"An F-150." Made sense now.

"Yeah. It rang a bell. I went back to the security recordings."

A cold hand squeezed JC's gut. "You saw it?"

"It arrived at the dealership about ten minutes before Daniel Kaufman's Lexus. We weren't looking for it. It belonged to the dealership."

Fuck, fuck, fuck.

He took a deep breath. "All three of them were there. Good catch. Call Dispatch. Have patrol find that truck. Owen left the church in it about ten minutes ago."


"Put the gun down," a male voice said.

Maddie peered around the headstone, and nearly wept with relief. Frank stood a dozen yards behind Ryan. His cowboy hat shaded his face but authority circled him in a tangible aura.

Ryan jerked and spun. He poked the pistol at Frank. "Get the hell out of here."

The gun wavered wildly in his shaking hand.

"What seems to be the problem?" Frank's voice sounded reasonable, conversational even. Like he was asking Ryan to sit down and have a beer.

"I'll shoot you." Rage—and fear—flew from Ryan's lips with his spittle.

"You don't want to do that." Frank's left fingertips flexed, like he was telling Maddie to ease away while Ryan was distracted.

She rose to a crouch and carefully keeping the monument between Ryan and herself, tiptoed to the next group of headstones.

"I will." Ryan took a step toward Frank.

The sirens were closer, converging from multiple directions.

"You have a wife. Kids who love you. You care about them, right?"

"Of course I do."

"They need you. Put the gun down. It won't solve anything."

Detective Dimitrak's car screeched into the parking lot. He bolted from the car, seemed to take in the situation and slowed to an amble. "Ryan. I hoped to talk to you before you left the church."

Ryan's hand—and the gun—jerked frantically, pointing first at one and then the other man. "Get away from me. I'll shoot."

"You were trying to help your brother." The detective stopped near Frank. "We understand. You couldn't turn him in."

What? The detective made it sound like it was A-Okay to help a murderer.

"Put the gun down. Between the three of us, we can figure out what to do next."

"It was her." Ryan spun around, his head jerking from side to side as if he were looking for her. "She did it. The poker chip. She had it."

Seriously? Did he really think anyone was going

174

to believe that lie at this point? Maddie saw Frank tense, like he was going to tackle Ryan. The detective shook his head and Frank eased back. Behind them, more police cars poured into the parking lot.

"We can deal with her later. Right now, we need your help to keep Owen from panicking."

Ryan twisted back to face the men. "Why should I?"

"You'd know the best way to handle him. You're his big brother. You know what to do." Detective Dimitrak took a step toward Ryan. "Just put the gun on the ground. Right there by your feet. We can sort this out."

Police officers had taken up positions surrounding the trio, but the detective acted as if he and Ryan were the only people present. Damn, he must have nerves of steel.

Ryan wavered, then his arm dropped as if the wires holding it up had broken. The gun tumbled onto the grass. In a flash, Detective Dimitrak had kicked the gun away, dropped Ryan to the ground, and slapped handcuffs on his wrists.

Uniformed officers converged on the pair. Two flanked Ryan as they dragged him to a patrol car.

The detective approached Frank and said something. Wow, for once they aren't growling at each other. At least one good thing came out of this mess.

The men shook hands and Frank walked over to join the other police officers.

Detective Dimitrak turned and crossed the lawn to where she huddled beside the tombstone. He held out a hand and helped her to her feet. "Are you okay?"

She nodded, not sure her voice would work.

"Dickerman." He gestured to one of the uniformed officers. "Bring me the first aid kit."

Seconds later, he wiped the blood from her cheek and examined the cut. "Just a scratch."

"Is it over? Did you arrest him?" She gingerly patted her check.

"This will take a while to process."

She wasn't sure if he meant mentally process what had happened or process the crime scene. "What about Owen?"

"We'll find him."

"Maddie!"

They turned toward the noise. A man dashed around the uniformed officer who had blocked his path.

The detective quirked an eyebrow. "Something I should know about?"

The first smile of the day cracked her face. "I'll let you know after we figure that out."

# EPILOGUE

*Months later*

Isn't it odd what money can do to people? Or rather, what they allow it to do to them?

Ryan forfeited his portion of the estate. Under Washington state law, when he helped Owen cover up the murder, he was treated as if he'd also pulled the trigger. He'd tried to commit suicide after he was arrested. Now he was in jail, awaiting trial. The only question seemed to be whether he'd go completely crazy or succeed in killing himself. Once Emily learned he'd been an accomplice to his father's murder, including drugging her as a backup alibi, she'd packed up the children and left.

Jessica also left Pasco the moment the estate paid out. Since Chris had cooperated with the police— he'd actually believed Ryan's adultery story and his "confession" had led to Ryan's arrest—he wasn't in jail for murder. He'd made a deal and served a short sentence. He lost his job with the airline, but with the millions Jess inherited, they could start over somewhere else.

Owen.

Maddie shook her head. Owen was still in the wind. Daniel had kept cash in the house—thousands for his "local" gambling. Owen had taken the money and run. The police found the pickup truck abandoned in Ellensburg. They suspected he bought a used car with part of the cash and vanished into a neighboring state. They'd find him eventually. Owen wasn't smart enough to stay hidden on his own.

Jeremy had quietly deposited money into an account for him. She suspected it was for an attorney. Not so much to keep Owen out of jail but rather to make sure he couldn't claim later that he didn't have competent counsel.

Not that she was cynical about Owen or anything.

She'd asked Jeremy about it once.

"I have more than I need and everything I want. Why not share?"

He was also anonymously contributing to local charities.

He'd moved back into his parents' house and spent part of his days painting and fixing it up. Nights, he still worked for the railroad. The rest of his time he spent with her and her son.

"Do it again, Jer'my." Caden laughed with delight as Jeremy swung him high in the air.

Maddie watched her son run around the backyard. She'd been cautious about introducing Jeremy to Caden, not wanting her son hurt by another disappearing man.

Asher, the original disappearing dad, had resurfaced long enough to demand part of Daniel's money. She suspected both Detective Dimitrak and Jeremy had told him to grow up and go get a job. Whatever else he might've said, the detective had been great about enforcing the restraining order against Asher. Her ex hadn't bothered her again.

Jeremy faked a flying tackle and tumbled onto the grass. Caden flung himself onto his chest. "I win!"

Her son was still her number one priority. He was thriving, loving her more predictable schedule and the stability Jeremy offered.

She need not have worried about letting Jeremy spend time with her son. He took to parenting like he'd been waiting for the chance all his life and Caden loved him.

Jeremy hadn't said the words yet, but his actions proved it every day.

Ryan's words from the funeral echoed in her memory. "You're the most unlucky person in the world."

He was wrong. She was the luckiest person in the world.

With Daniel's generosity, she was going to school full time.

Because of his generous inheritance, she had enough money to buy a new car—a new to her car anyway. With the money in the trust fund for tuition, she'd been able to cut her working hours to have more time with her son.

And for Daniel's son.

Because that was the real reason she was the luckiest person.

She had people in her life she loved and people who loved her.

**Thank you for reading** *Double Down*!

**If you enjoyed Maddie and JC's story:**

**Review it.** Tell other readers why you liked this book by reviewing it at Amazon, Barnes & Noble, iBooks, or Kobo. Goodreads is another excellent review site.

**Read another one of my books.**
For more information, please visit my website http://cperkinswrites.com

**Want advance notice for my next release?** Stop by and sign up for the new release announcement newsletter on my website or Facebook page.

Thanks for reading!
Cathy


**Coming soon:**

*The Rockcrawler Book*, second in the Holly Price Mystery series

# ABOUT THE AUTHOR

An award-winning author, Cathy Perkins works in the financial industry, where she's observed the hide-in-plain-sight skills employed by her villains. She writes predominantly financial-based mysteries but enjoys exploring the relationship aspect of her characters' lives.

When not writing, she can be found doing battle with the beavers over the pond height or setting off on another travel adventure. Born and raised in South Carolina, she now lives in Washington with her husband, children, several dogs and the resident deer herd.

For more about Cathy Perkins:

| | |
|---|---|
| Website | www.cperkinswrites.com |
| Facebook | CathyPerkinsAuthor |
| Twitter | @cperkinswrites |
| Email | cathy@cperkinswrites.com |

# SO ABOUT THE MONEY

**EXCERPT:** Meet Holly Price and JC Dimitrak:

The irritating *brittz* of the doorbell—another item on her long list of Things To Replace—interrupted [Holly's argument with Alex Montoya.]

"You expecting somebody?" Alex asked.

"I hope it isn't a reporter." Shaking her head, she crossed the room. "If my mom heard about this…"

She pushed the curtain aside, peeked through the long sidelight window and recoiled.

No reporter.

No mother.

JC Dimitrak stood on her doorstep.

She didn't know why she was surprised. She'd known he'd show up eventually, but *now*? This soon?

He dipped his head in greeting. Even tired and grim-faced, he still looked better than sex on a stick.

Where did *that* come from? She scrambled to pull her thoughts together and opened the door.

*Wait a minute,* her inner teenager shrieked. *I'm not ready.*

"May I come in?"

"What are you doing here? I mean, at my house?"

"Remember the 'Can we do this later?' part?"

Stepping back, she widened the opening. JC wore the same dark slacks and heavy coat he'd had on at the game management area. He unbuttoned his overcoat, revealing the huge pistol clamped to his belt beside his badge. This man—this *stranger*, she reminded herself, because she didn't know him anymore—was definitely a leader. He had the commanding presence, backed by more than a hint of sex appeal.

He'd always had it.

Only now he was armed. And undoubtedly dangerous.

"I take it this is an official visit," she said.

He ignored the observation, and instead gave her yoga pants, T-shirt, and wet hair a slow inspection. The twitch of his eyebrow and assessing glance told her he knew she wasn't wearing a bra.

Alex moved into the foyer. "Why are you here?"

JC glanced at Alex. Sex assumptions hung like a cartoon balloon over his head. For a moment, something that might've been anger or jealousy tightened his face. Then it vanished. "Did I catch you at a bad time?"

She said, "No" at the same time Alex said, "Yes."

"Glad we cleared that up." JC's smile didn't reach his eyes. "I need to get your statement, Holly. Before you take off again."

She propped her fist on her hip. "You know, the way I remember things, *you* walked out."

"Don't go there, Holly. You don't know the first thing about me."

"I know everything that matters."

Alex stepped up. "We've both done everything we can to cooperate, but quit hiding behind your badge. If you have a problem with Holly, you should bow out of the investigation."

JC gave him a cool examination. "I need to talk to each of you. Alone. We can do that at the station, if you'd prefer."

"No way. I'm not going to the police station

183

without a lawyer," Alex said.

"You can leave."

Wow. She *really* hadn't thought the day could get any worse. "Guys. Break." She jammed her fingers into a time-out "T."

"Maybe we should call Phil Brewer." Alex folded his arms across his chest in universal male posturing position.

While he got points for trying to defend her, she rejected his choice with, "Phil does corporate work."

Alex glared at the detective. "He'd still know how to make this guy quit harassing you."

JC didn't say a word, but behind his stiff face he seemed to be enjoying stirring the pot.

"Stop. He isn't harassing me." Weirding her out, yes. Harassing, no. She knew what that felt like. Right now, JC might be doing the über-cop routine, but if the tension got any hotter, they could roast marshmallows. And nobody was going to sing "Kumbaya."

"Alex." She touched his arm, finally moving his attention off the detective. "I'm tired. I'd rather get this over with. Go on to the restaurant. I'll be okay."

For one long moment, she was afraid he was going to push the issue.

With a sharp snort of irritation, he turned, strode across the room, and grabbed his jacket. Thrusting his arms into the sleeves, he headed for the door. He made a move like he intended to kiss her.

She froze. The oh-God-not-in-front-of-my-mother cringe warred with the in-your-face-JC snub.

And from the half-smile on JC's face, he'd caught her hesitation, even if Alex didn't seem to notice.

"I'll call you in a little while." *To make sure JC's gone*, bristled from his scowl. Alex brushed his lips across hers and vanished through the front door.

Alrighty.

JC Dimitrak.

She drew in a deep breath. "What do you want to know?"

He crossed the foyer. His hard soles rapped against the bare subfloor. "Love what you've done with the place."

Silently counting to ten, she decided to interpret the comment as a compliment, although he clearly hadn't intended it that way. "I'm working on it. The guy who used to own the house opened up the interior. I don't know what they were thinking back in the 70s, but the original house completely ignored the view, which is its best feature. It had those narrow, clerestory windows that kinda remind me of bunker openings."

She stared at the living room's new, oversized panes and forced her mouth to close. Babbling wasn't going to keep them from talking about Marcy.

Talking about Marcy's dead body would make her murder so much more real.

"What'd he do? Get in over his head?"

"The guy who owned it? Yeah. The bank foreclosed."

JC gestured at the buckets and painting supplies. "Weekend project?"

"I planned to paint." She wasn't sure what to make of his tone or the question. Was he assuming she was a cold-hearted bitch for planning to paint *today*, the day she'd found a friend's body?

Well, she already knew where he stood on the bitch-meter, but he could've at least asked *when* she set out the paint instead of figuring she was breaking out the roller *today*.

She planned to paint because it was normal. Because it was what normal people did. Normal people whose friends weren't dead.

No way was she admitting any of that.

"The carpet installer's scheduled for next week. He recommended I paint before he replaces the rug."

They both glanced at the hideous shag carpet.

"Good idea." A grin tugged at JC's mouth.

She bit her lip to keep from smiling—the shag was truly awful—but the tension in the room dropped by ten degrees.

He looked at her, studying her expression. "Actually, I'm impressed you took on the renovation."

She raised an eyebrow.

"I thought you said you'd never live in Richland again."

"You heard what you wanted to hear." One of the reasons they'd broken up was he'd wanted a stay-at-home wife, stuck behind a picket fence. She'd had no interest in playing the Stepford Wife role. Any chance they'd had of creating *any* kind of home crashed and burned when she came home from college after one of their arguments—about her being in Seattle and her plans to stay there after graduation—and found him with another woman.

But here she was, in Richland.

With a house.

An empty house.

Whatever.

"The house is an investment. Most of my friends think I'm nuts for renovating it myself."

His lips tightened around a smile.

If she didn't know him, she'd have missed it. One of the things he'd loved about her—*said* he'd loved—

was her tendency to throw herself into projects other people thought were crazy. She always pulled them off, though.

"This place *is* butt-ugly on the outside, but you have to admit the view is stunning." *Keep him focused on the externals.* The last thing she wanted was for him to look at her too closely. To see inside her the way he used to.

JC didn't need to know she loved the ugly little house. Everything about the house and the renovation was tangible. Did she fix the water heater or not? Get the room painted or not? There were none of the murky gray areas like there were in the rest of her life, where maybe she succeeded—or maybe she didn't.

He moved past her to the window, then turned and leaned against the wall. "I heard you were back."

She gave him an *and-your-point-is*? look. What had he expected? That she'd call him? Show up on *his* cheating, black-hearted doorstep?

"Why'd you move back to Richland?"

She wasn't going to tell him her father had suffered a midlife brain fart and taken off with his yoga instructor, or that she'd made a deal with her mother to bail out the family accounting business, a decision she regretted on practically a daily basis. And at a deeper level, his question pissed her off because he knew damn well *exactly* why she was there. She'd seen the cop powwow information exchange out at Big Flats, where the deputies had brought JC up to speed. All he was doing now was digging for personal information.

She crossed her arms and ignored the way her body heated up just because he was in the room. Stupid body. If it heated up, it was because she was mad. Period. "You know why I moved. And if you were really interested, it would take you about two seconds to find out when I changed the address on my driver's license from Seattle to Richland."

He smiled and two dimples appeared.

She caught her breath. Oh, man. How could she have forgotten about his dimples?

It didn't matter how many times she told herself they were just a simple indentation of flesh. Dimples made serious, grown-up men look like they still had a mischievous little boy inside. The kind who sledded down the forbidden steepest slopes, dyed the dog green for St. Patty's Day, or knew how to be especially devilish in bed.

And she personally knew every one of those items applied to JC.

In spite of her irritation, she smiled at him and his grin widened. His shoulders relaxed and his eyes grew a shade warmer. "You never could pass up a chance to jerk my chain."

"You set yourself up often enough."

Why was he making nice? She did the mental head-slap. *What was she thinking?* JC stood for "Just Cool" as often as it did "Just Crazy."

"Is this your loosen-up-the-idiot routine, so I'll say something stupid like, 'I killed Marcy'?"

His face immediately closed off, but before he could make another comment, she pulled on the composed shell she used at the negotiating table. "Look. At least for tonight, let's declare a truce. You quit taking jabs at me and I won't take any swipes at you. I'll tell you everything I know about Marcy."

He pushed away from the wall and nodded. "Sounds good to me."

"If we're going to talk about her, I need coffee." She headed toward the kitchen.

JC followed her into the large area beyond the vacant living room. "Nice."

There was no snark in his tone this time.

She surveyed the renovated space with pride. A tile-topped peninsula—she'd set every one of those suckers—separated the kitchen from the dining area. Cherry cabinets lined the interior walls and surrounded the Bosch appliances. City lights sparkled through the oversized windows at night, but right now she could see eighty miles to the Blue Mountains.

"Have a seat." She pulled out coffee and filled the machine. "With all that activity at Big Flats, I'm surprised you're here. Shouldn't you be following leads or something?"

From the safety of distance, she gave him a closer examination. His hair was shorter. No big surprise there, he *was* a policeman. His face was tanned; apparently he still spent time outdoors. The lines at the corners of his eyes were new. He'd filled out, not that he'd been a wimp when she knew him. She checked out the broad chest and shoulders tapering to slim hips and remembered why hormones had fried her brain when she was in college.

Good thing she was too smart for that now.

All his assets still didn't outweigh the big ol' blot in his liability column, a.k.a. infidelity.

He dropped his coat on a counter stool, but claimed the chair at the head of the table. "You looked like you were nearly out on your feet earlier, so I let you go home." A lazy smile, the kind that used to set her heart racing, warmed his expression. "You still look good, though."

"Hmm." Telling her pulse and her traitorous hormones to go take another cold shower, she gave her

189

CATHY PERKINS

ratty yoga pants and T-shirt an appraising glance. She didn't have to see her hair to know it had already dried in the desert air without benefit of blow-dryer, styling gel, or flatiron. "What do you want, JC?"

He laughed.

It was the belly-deep, I'm-an-idiot-and-you-called-me-on-it combined with I-don't-take-myself-too-seriously chuckle she remembered. One of the protective barriers holding in her anger and hurt creaked a little, as though it was rusty and maybe she didn't need it anymore.

*No, no, no.* He was *not* getting under her skin.

The coffee machine made steamy brewing noises behind her. Deliberately turning her back on him and his smile, she picked up his coat and headed toward the closet. As she draped the garment over a wooden hanger, her nose caught floral perfume wafting from the wool. Definitely not JC's cologne.

Her stomach knotted. She should've known there'd be a woman in his life.

Anger knifed through any remaining illusions. She knew better than to trust anything he said or did. But what did he think he was doing, giving her that *c'mon* look?

She slapped the hanger onto the closet rod. He wasn't wearing a ring. Was he still married to what's-her-face? Like being married stopped anybody. Look at Dad. If he fell off the rails, why should she expect JC to be different?

She already *knew* JC wasn't different.

She returned to the kitchen and slammed around a few coffee mugs. She wasn't sure if she was mad at her father, JC, or herself for still being even the tiniest little bit attracted to him.

190

*Damn* him.

He had a notepad open on the table. "I have some questions."

"Well, we can keep this short and I'll start painting. Here are all the answers." She ticked them off on her fingers. "I thought we were going hiking. I had no idea it was opening weekend for pheasant hunting. I had no idea Marcy's body was in that swampy area. And no, I didn't kill her. Would you like your coffee in a to-go cup?

All business now, he leveled a stare at her she figured was supposed to be intimidating, but the assorted investment bankers, venture capitalists, and arrogant attorneys she'd dealt with in Seattle had made her immune to that kind of nonsense. JC was an amateur compared to them.

"Don't be a bitch, Holly. It doesn't suit you."

She pressed her hands onto the counter and managed to keep her expression neutral. She wished she could control the warmth climbing her cheeks. She'd known those dimpled signals were just a crappy ploy. Nobody turned it off and on like that if it was real. "Dammit JC, quit jerking me around. I'll do whatever I can to help you find Marcy's killer, but I don't know what I can say that'll make any difference."

"You knew Ms. Ramirez. What can you tell me about her? What was she like?"

Holly pulled in a deep breath. *Do it for Marcy.*

"So the body is definitely Marcy's?"

He nodded, but didn't elaborate.

"Damn. I'd hoped..." The tiny spark of hope she'd harbored vanished and left the world a little darker.

With a sigh, she leaned against the counter and thought about the woman who'd become her friend. "Marcy works—worked—across the hall at Stevens

Ventures. She was fun, outgoing. We did lunch, happy hour at Bookwalter, that kind of thing. We had different backgrounds, but we just clicked, you know?"

The coffeemaker sputtered behind her.

"I liked her. I wish I'd gotten a chance to know her better." She stared at the floor before raising her gaze to meet his. "I can't believe she's dead. Who would want to kill her? Why?"

"That's what I'm trying to figure out. Do you know who Ms. Ramirez was dating?"

"I wish I could be more help, but I don't know much about her personal life."

"I thought you were friends."

"We are…were." Holly lifted a shoulder. "She never talked about a boyfriend. I think she was seeing someone, but like I said… "

"Do you know anybody who'd want to hurt her?"

"I can't think of anybody. She was so…nice." Holly chewed her lower lip, frustrated with her explanation. "I'm not doing a very good job telling you about her. What she was like, as a person. Marcy…loved pretty clothes. And she loved to dance. You should've seen her. She could move like the music came from inside her, and if she was dancing with somebody—"

"She dance with anybody in particular?"

Holly blinked. The memory of the dance floor where she'd admired Marcy's footwork vanished, and she returned to a grim-faced cop who wanted to know if one of her friends had killed the woman. No way was she going to say Alex and Marcy should've auditioned for that dance show together. Alex had been her date when they went dancing, not Marcy's. "Nobody in particular."

"So no known enemies?"

"Not that I know of." She removed a spoon from a drawer. "Do you think this was a random violence thing? You know, wrong time, wrong place?"

"It's possible."

"How'd she end up out at the Snake River?"

"We seem to have this backward—I ask the questions and you answer them."

"Then ask a question I know the answer to." She thought about Marcy's body ending up at Big Flats while she returned to the coffeemaker and filled the mugs. "If she knew her killer, she might've gone out to the river to meet him. Or maybe the bad guy took her there."

"And you don't know anybody she'd meet out there."

"No."

She left her coffee black, but reached into the refrigerator for milk. She added some to JC's mug along with a healthy scoop of sugar.

"Sorry, no cream." She placed the drink in front of him.

JC stared at the mug, then cocked his head to look at her. "You remember how I like my coffee." His eyes were warm and friendly. Gold flecks lightened the brown depths.

He had beautiful eyes. She'd gotten lost in them once.

Her breathing hitched. There was more in his eyes than warmth.

*Longing.*

*Regret.*

A shiny sphere swelled, as delicate and gossamer as a child's blown bubble. Hope? Happiness?

*Love?*

Time rewound and they were six years younger,

madly in love, and spending every possible minute together. Memories of times and places she'd brought him coffee surged through her. Seattle's Best, study breaks. Her dorm, his apartment, tangled sheets. Hot coffee, hotter kisses.

She slammed the gate on memory lane. He'd made his choice. "It's only coffee. I thought all cops like coffee."

He blinked at her flat tone. His gaze dropped to the notebook. "You stated you went to lunch with Ms. Ramirez. Who else went with you? What did you talk about?"

It was his official voice, cool and impersonal. *Good. Let's keep this purely professional.*

She pulled out a chair and sat down. "Marcy's sister, Yessica, went with us. Occasionally, someone else from the office came."

Sipping coffee for fortification, she told him the basics, the people they ran around with, the places they went. "One thing I *do* know. Marcy hated the Great Outdoors. She would never, ever have been near Big Flats by her own choice."

JC scribbled notes. "Where were you last Tuesday?"

She nearly spewed coffee. "Do you actually think I killed my friend?"

His face was expressionless. "Answer the question."

Stunned he'd even *remotely* consider her a possible murderer, her hands rose and fell in an incredulous gesture. "At work. At meetings."

"Can you be more specific?"

"I don't remember exactly, but it'll be on my work calendar."

"I'll need a copy of your schedule. Ms. Ramirez disappeared on Tuesday, according to her sister. The ME estimated time of death as Tuesday evening. I need to know where you were during that time period."

Her jaw dropped. "You're serious."

His eyes didn't waver. "I wouldn't have asked if I weren't."

"Do I need an attorney?"

He jotted a note on his paper. "Anything different happen last week? Before her sisters reported her missing?"

Holly stalled by taking another sip of coffee. Should she call a lawyer? She eyed JC over the rim of her mug. In spite of the way things ended between them, she still believed he'd play fair. And she hadn't said anything he could twist around—except some personal innuendo he couldn't use against her.

With a sigh, she placed her mug on a coaster and hoped she was being helpful and not naïve. "At first, we thought Yessica was overreacting. Marcy hadn't been gone a day and her sister was acting like Bigfoot had stomped out of the Cascades and dragged her home to his cave."

Warmth again flooded her face. "I didn't mean that the way it sounded. Obviously, she was right to be worried. It's just that Marcy had taken off before, so the rest of us weren't really concerned."

"When? Any idea where she went?"

"Marcy took off earlier this fall, said she wanted to be by herself. She made it real clear she didn't want to talk about it." Holly shrugged. "When she took off this time, our receptionist talked to the Stevens Ventures receptionist. Marcy had told her she was going away with her boyfriend. And no, I don't know who she meant."

"Nothing like firsthand information." JC lifted a derisive eyebrow. "I never knew you to listen to gossip."

"Hey, you asked. You're the frikkin' detective. You go figure out who killed her. Just be damned sure you put in your report it wasn't me."

For a long moment, JC stared at her. Then he closed the folio, laid his pen on the table, and folded his arms across his chest. Eyes narrowed, his expression reflected a mental debate. Knowing him, mostly likely it was whether to treat her like a suspect, a witness, or an ex-girlfriend. "I expected more cooperation from you."

She mimicked his body language—stiff back, squared shoulders, minus the glare. "I *am* cooperating. I answered every one of your questions."

"The whole time I've been here, you've said a lot of words, but everything you've told me adds up to a big fat zero." His tone was level, coolly devoid of emotion. "I have to ask myself, why is she being so evasive?"

"Wha..?" She sputtered with outrage, but he cut her off with a slashing hand motion.

"Tell me, Holly. What am I supposed to think? You and your boyfriend *just happen* to find the murdered body of a woman who is your friend and his partner's employee. Interesting coincidence?"


I hope you enjoyed reading this excerpt from *So About The Money*.

Made in the USA
Columbia, SC
12 November 2018